FAIRY TALES
FROM
THE BROTHERS GRIMM

THE BROTHERS GRIMM AND ERIK FORREST JACKSON

ILLUSTRATED BY OWEN RICHARDSON

Penguin Workshop

An Imprint of Penguin Random House

TABLE OF CONTENTS

Prologue

In the middle of the commotion, Scooter raps his knuckles on the back of the clipboard he's clutching to his chest. Considering the ruckus that everyone's making, and considering his exceedingly soft fingers, the gesture doesn't have much impact. With an exasperated sigh, he turns to Kermit for help. The frog climbs up onto a nearby wooden chair and shouts, "Hey, everybody!" Still no response, so Kermit turns to a shaggy short guy passing by. "Hey, Animal," he pleads. "Could I get a little help here?"

Animal eagerly bounds up onto the chair and bellows: "Quiiiiii-eeeeeet!!!"

Well, that sure gets their attention, and in the silence that follows, Kermit cheerfully announces, "Five minutes till we start!"

The momentary quiet ends, erupting into a clamor as, around them, all manner of creatures frantically prep for the adventurous production ahead: a decidedly

Muppet spin on eighteen enduring folktales collected and preserved by an enterprising pair of German brothers. Among the unorthodox sights before Kermit and Scooter are a blond flower child in caftan and Birkenstocks who's collapsing to the floor in a pretend, poison-induced stupor; a wedge of cheese and a blob of chopped liver running lines together; and, curled up on a sofa, a lazy snaggletoothed goat somehow dozing through it all.

Amid this, Kermit joins Scooter in helping Pepé the King Prawn locate a missing costume. Finally spying the ensemble on a clothing rack, Kermit passes it to the gangly crustacean. "You'd better hurry and get changed," urges the frog.

Scooter points to his watch and adds, "It's four minutes until the first story, and you've got a big part in it!"

"Doan rush me, okay?" replies a nonchalant Pepé. "Haven't I been telling you for an hour that I'll be ready in a minute?" He puts a hand on Kermit's shoulder and leans in. "Pepé has been studying the meditation, and one thing I learn is that rushing is no good for you. Because while is true the early bird may get the worm, is also true the second rodent gets the cheese."

Nearby, and clearly within earshot, Rizzo the Rat pumps a fist in the air and cheers, "That's *right*, he does!"

Pepé stares earnestly into Kermit's eyes. "You are too

stressed, okay, and could use the help. Are you ready for wisdoms?" Kermit nods. Pepé intones: "As the wise man once said to me, 'Do the opposite of whatever I tell you, okay.' *So I didn't.*"

He lets the words hang in the air for a moment, then raises an eyebrow knowingly and saunters off.

Kermit is still scratching his head at the prawn's words when he notices a look of concern worrying Scooter's face. "What's wrong?"

The stage manager glances both ways, then whispers to Kermit, "Has anyone broken the news to Tom, Dick, and Harry that they're not going to be in this book?"

"Tom, Dick, and Harry . . . ," says Kermit, trying to place the names. "Oh! Is that the three-headed monster whose footsteps don't make any sound?" Scooter nods yes.

"Gosh," says Kermit, "I thought *you* were taking care of that."

"Taking care of what?" asks Tom, Dick, and Harry, who had somehow just appeared without a sound right behind them.

"Uhhhh," stammers Scooter.

"How do they *do* that?" marvels Kermit.

Before anyone can answer, Miss Piggy struts over in her white karate outfit and says, "Scooter, I'm sorry I'm tardy, but my martial arts class ran late. We were learning to break boards in half."

"Hey, that's groovy," says Janice from down by Piggy's feet and fresh from a fake faint. She lifts up on one elbow. "Like, now you'll be able to protect yourself the next time a board attacks?"

"As I was saying," Piggy continues to Scooter, "if you could just point me in the direction of the private dressing room reserved exclusively for *moi*."

"Well," Scooter croaks, his throat suddenly very dry in the demanding diva's presence, "there are nearly a hundred of us Muppets appearing in these stories, so space is awful tight around here."

Piggy blinks three times then says slowly through a frozen smile, "I do not understand how that pertains to *moi*."

Scooter swallows hard and looks to Kermit for help.

"You see, Piggy," begins the frog in soothing tones, "you definitely have a private dressing room . . . though it's not so much a dressing room as it is a storage room . . . and instead of it being private, it's being shared by, well, everyone." The diva's impending outburst is interrupted when a blue blur crashes through the ceiling and hits the floor next to them with a resounding thud.

"Gonzo!" cries Scooter as the fuzzy daredevil crawls

out from beneath his cape and dusts himself off.

Kermit eyes the hole in the ceiling. "Were you skydiving?"

"Not exactly. I call it 'cannonballing,'" Gonzo clarifies. "It's skydiving without a parachute."

Kermit's jaw drops. "You jumped out of a plane with no parachute?!"

"Aww," he counters with a dismissive flick of the wrist, "that's the easy part."

"So what's the hard part?"

"Hitting the ground." He rubs his shoulder. "But I guarantee you I'll stick that landing eventually. What's that old saying? 'Thirty-third time's the charm'?"

Two elderly gents in three-piece suits stand a few paces away, scowling. "You know, Gonzo," says the one called Statler, "my nickname for you is 'the *Venus de Milo*.'"

Gonzo cocks his head. "Why's that?"

"Because you're not all there!"

"That's for certain," says Statler's old pal Waldorf. "I've got my own name for him: 'peanut brittle.'"

"Why 'peanut brittle'?"

"Because he's half nuts!" They both break into mirthful chortles.

"Aw gee, guys," says Gonzo, blushing a deeper shade

of blue, "this is no time for compliments, the stories are about to start!" And off he goes to change into costume.

Meanwhile, as the stagehand Beauregard and his assistant penguins hammer away at various set pieces, an urgent and outraged voice cuts through the crowd noise. *"Have you read this?!"* Beau, the birds, and all the rest stop what they're doing and turn to see Sam Eagle marching across the room holding a sheaf of pages aloft in an upraised wing. The big blue raptor is visibly livid, his unibrow deeply furrowed. "Have you actually read these twisted, bizarre, and violent tales that you're all about to appear in? Is this your idea of good, wholesome entertainment? Children being swallowed alive? Creatures tearing themselves in two? These stories are a hundred percent indecent!"

Waldorf scoffs. "And when was the last time the Muppets did anything even fifty percent decent?"

The bird thinks for a moment. "Point taken."

"Look, Sam," says Kermit, "they're just stories, and the Muppets are born storytellers. These are some of the most beloved tales in the world, passed down for generations. They're the inspiration for countless books and movies, and they've been translated into more than a hundred and sixty languages."

"*Globalism!* Harrumph!"

But before Sam can declare another harrumph, Scooter swiftly adds, "We were actually counting on you to be in one or two of them with us."

"Oh—what? Really? You want *me* to be in them?"

The eagle is clearly quite flattered, so the stage manager forges ahead, handing him some pages from his clipboard. "Here are the three we've got you slated for."

Sam glances at their titles and recoils. "But these are some of the most objectionable stories of the whole lot! Terrible things happen in them!"

Kermit chimes in. "These plots are pure make-believe, a marvelous mixture of allegories, metaphors, and symbols."

A loud crash from the corner makes them all turn. "CYMBALS!" yells Animal, who's seated at his drum set. He bashes the high hat gleefully with his drumsticks.

Scooter checks his watch. "Oh boy, it's go time!"

"Then we've got the perfect transition," says Kermit. "Animal, can you give us a drumroll?" The shaggy percussionist nods his head vigorously, then pounds a thunderous tattoo on the bass drum as the narrator takes a deep breath, ready to begin . . . just as soon as you turn the page.

We're waiting.

You can turn the page NOW.

Camillarella

AFTER "ASHPUTTEL"

Once upon a time . . . long, long ago . . . last Monday . . . there was a rich Scotsman whose wife took ill. Their devoted daughter, Camilla, a fetching young chicken with a gentle demeanor and fine white feathers, roosted by her mother's bedside day and night.

That morning, the chick overheard the doctor tell her father in solemn tones, "Well, Angus McGonagle," for that was her father's name, "the prognosis isn't good." They were talking about her mother's future, because there apparently wasn't going to be much of it.

After the doc left, the ailing lady mustered up the strength to stammer, "Always be . . . a good girl . . . my little Camillarella," which was her pet name for her daughter, "and I will look down from heaven . . . and watch over you . . . but not in a creepy way." Then she kicked the bucket.

A moment later, her mother asked in a weak voice, "Who put that bucket so close to the bed?"

When Camilla's mom actually *did* pass away, she was planted in the backyard garden, right between the peas and the peppers. The little chicken went every day past the swing set and swimming pool to the grave and weeded and wept and ate the occasional earthworm, and she was always good and kind to everyone, just as her mother had implored.

Time passed. The snow fell. Britney Spears had another comeback, fell from favor yet again, and came back once more. But Camilla always made her daily visits to the spot, and by the time the spring arrived, her father, a big-featured purple gent of gargoyle heritage, had gotten hitched again. Angus's new wife, a pleasingly plump glamour-puss called Miss Piggy, brought with her two kids of her own, Andy and Randy. Some might say these, uh, daughters were decent lookers, with their pale pink skin, pointy ears, and supersize snouts, but inside they were unquestionably selfish and arrogant.

"I object!" said Andy to Randy.

"Because they called us selfish and arrogant?" asked Randy.

"No, that's accurate. I object to us having to play *girls* in this story—we're *boys*!"

"Well, that's not a problem. Good actors can play anything."

"Yeah, and the problem is that we're terrible actors."

Piggy realized the jig was up and confessed: "Look, I'll level with you. Scooter tried to get Betina and Belinda Cratchit for these parts, but they're booked in Reno. You have to take one for the team."

So with the arrival of Piggy and her two "daughters," there began a very sorry stretch for poor little Camilla. One night at dinner, Andy said with a sneer, "It's so yucky how that feather-face eats food through her nose!"

Randy, who at that moment was digging a finger in his own, jeered, "Yeah, *gross!*"

Camilla cowered and skulked out of the room.

You might wonder about the poor chick's father at this point. Angus McGonagle had remained oblivious to the changes taking place in the household, blinded as he was by his love for Piggy (and here we are contractually obligated to make note of her mellifluous voice™, mesmerizing blue eyes™, and lustrous honey locks™).

The self-centered stepmother was no help, either. She focused only on her phone, obsessed with her Twitter feed. "I just got retweeted by Dwayne 'The Rock' Johnson," she once bragged to an empty room.

Neither parent paid attention when Andy and Randy banished Camilla from the dinner table, or hid her fine clothes and gave her only an old gray frock to put on, or laughed at her and treated her like the scullery maid. She was forced to do all the hard work, rising even before daylight to bring the water, to wash the clothes, to cold-press Piggy's juices.

Besides that, Andy and Randy plagued her in all sorts of other ways, from putting Pop Rocks in her grain to egging her in the yard with her own eggs. They frequently made fun of her nervous clucking and mocked her spotty plumage (she couldn't help it—it was molting season). On the evenings when she was exhausted, which was every evening, she had no cushy hay to roost in, but was made to lie among the ashes on the stones by the hearth. This, of course, made her always dusty and dirty, so her stepsiblings made up names for her.

"*Ash*-ley," shouted Randy. "Get it? She's covered in ashes."

Andy chimed in with one of his own: "*Soot*-zanne!"

"*Ember*-ly!"

"*Burn*-adette!"

Piggy had tried to tune out their brainless banter but could hold her tongue no longer. "You might want to try using the word *cinder—duh*."

"'Cinder-duh'?" asked Andy skeptically. "Is that even English?"

"Just *cinder*," said Piggy, with a roll of her eyes. "Use

the word *cinder* to make a name for her."

"There are zero names you could make using the word *cinder*," said Randy, shaking his head.

"Can't be done," agreed Andy.

"Impossible," concluded Randy. "Piggy, you're not very good at this, are you?"

Piggy shook her head. "If ignorance is bliss, why aren't you two happier?"

It was then that Angus announced he was taking a trip. The bagpipe enthusiast was planning to travel to a neighboring kingdom's annual wind-instrument convention. He asked Piggy's kids in his Scottish brogue, "Is there anythin' youse wee lasses would laik me to bring ya back from mah journey?"

"Video games!" said Randy.

"And any chocolate except M&M's!" said Andy.

"What's wrong with M&M's?" asked Angus.

"Too hard to peel."

"Aye, all right. And dear Camilla," said the father, "what would ya like, me lass?"

She thought for a moment, then whispered, *"Bawk b-gaw, bawk bawk b-gark."*

"What'd she say?" asked Randy with a scoff.

"She says she would laik the first twig that brushes 'gainst me tam-o'-shanter when I turn back toward home," Angus replied, pointing to his soft woolen plaid cap. "She is an awful simple gal." Randy and Andy looked at each other, marveling at such a silly request, and launched into guffaws.

After the convention ended and he'd piped to his heart's content, Angus bought for Piggy's oddball offspring the video games and chocolate they had asked for. On his return, as he steered his bike down a tree-lined path, a dangling twig brushed against his cap, so he snapped it off and tucked it into the pocket of his kilt.

When he got home and passed out the presents, Camilla graciously thanked him for the twig and promptly carried it in her orange beak to her mother's grave. There, she planted it in the soil, then cried so much that it was drenched with her tears. Like a magical beanstalk from another brand of fairy tales, it instantly sprouted and became a towering weeping willow. Three times every day she went to it and cried, saving Angus a bundle on the water bill.

One afternoon Camilla looked high into the willow's branches and was surprised to discover that something had built its nest there. But the critter that peered down over the side of the nest was surprisingly not of the winged variety. *"Hola,"* it said while waving with several of its four hands. "I think maybe you was expecting a bird in here, okay. But I am Pepé, and believe it or not, I am your Fairy Godprawn. I will do the watching over you and bring whatever it is you wish for, Camillarella."

Her heart jumped: *Camillarella!* Her mother's pet name! It was proof to her that this peculiar tree-nesting Spanish-speaking sea creature must indeed have been sent from heaven, and that maybe, just maybe, her bad-luck streak was over. (Don't count on it.)

Now it happened that the king of that land, a fine blue bachelor named The Great Gonzo, had planned a nightly feast and masquerade party, which was to last three days. By its end, he hoped to have found a bride.

"Uhhh, that doesn't make any sense," said Randy. "If he's looking to get hitched, why would he want the babes to wear masks?"

Andy chimed in: "'Cuz that way he'll fall for someone's inner beauty, not just a pretty face."

Piggy snorted. "'Inner beauty'? That's an oxymoron."

Randy laughed and punched Andy. "Ha ha! She thinks you're a moron."

Andy punched Randy. "She thinks *you're* a moron!"

"Not true," Piggy corrected with a sweet smile. "I think you're *both* morons."

That evening, the two young pigs made their stepchicken assist them as they prepared for the shindig.

Andy refused to say the next line of dialogue, so Randy, who *really* wanted to go to the party, delivered it instead: "Now, Camilla," he began, in stilted, actorly tones, breathing during only the most unnatural of spots, "come scrub behind our ears, shine our. Shoes, and tie our. Sashes for us, for we are going to dance. At the king's. Feast."

"Now you see why I didn't want to say it," Andy explained to the reader. "It sounds too ridiculous."

"Well, for this story we're supposed to be ridiculous," rationalized Randy.

"You're ridiculous."

"No, *you're* ridiculous."

"Take it from me," said Piggy, "you're *both* ridiculous! Now I've had enough of this bickering. We don't have much time until the party starts—so shake a tail feather, Camilla!"

The chicken did as she was told, briskly scrubbing them till their bristly pink hides glowed, and dolling them up in ribbons and bows. When she was finished, she begged her stepmother to let her attend as well. *"Vous?!"* said Piggy, so startled at the request that she actually looked up from her phone mid-tweet. *"Vous* who is covered in dust and dirt? *Vous* who have nothing to wear and who cannot even dance—*vous* want to go with *nous*?"

The bedraggled bird kept on begging, so Piggy at last marched downstairs to the kitchen and grabbed a box of grape-flavored Nerds from the counter. "Fine!" she said, silencing Camilla mid-*bawk* with a finger to the beak. "How about I throw these candies into the fireplace and *if* you can pick them out before an hour has passed, you can go to the feast, too." Her stepmother tossed the tiny purple nuggets down among the ashes (they blended in quite diabolically with the cinders) and marched off to give herself a manicure.

But the put-upon chick didn't despair. She had an idea. She scurried out the back door, skirted the pool, and went into the garden. At the base of the willow, she cried up to Pepé the Fairy Godprawn in his strange little shrimpy nest: *"Bawk b'gawk bawk bawk!"*

"Is true," he answered as he woke from his siesta and peered down through half-open lids. "I did say I would get you whatever you wish for. And a Fairy Godprawn always keep his word." With that, he hollered in the direction of the horizon, "Here, chickie, chickie, chickies!"

Camilla watched with wonder as a flock of chickens from the bordering property scampered over the hill, a wave of white feathers and wiggling red waddles. They arrived at the house chirping excitedly, fluttered into the kitchen, beelined for the fireplace, and set to work, pick-

pick-picking at the ashes with their beaks. They soon had plucked out all the Nerds and dropped them into a dish. Long before the end of the hour, the work was quite done. They flapped out again and returned over the hill to their coops.

Camilla, overjoyed that she would now be allowed to go to the ball, carefully carried the full dish in her outstretched wings and presented it to her stepmother, who was upstairs blowing on her wet fingernails and lounging with Andy and Randy. She saw hopeful Camilla and the plate of candies and immediately shook her head. "Nope, no way!" she said.

"Besides," Andy said, "you can't dance."

Randy said, "And you have no fancy clothes."

But Camilla didn't stop begging until Piggy returned to the kitchen, took down from the pantry a second box of Nerds, and shook them into the ashes along with the first plateful again. "Fine then," she said pertly. "If you can pick twice as many candy pieces out of the ashes before an hour has passed, you may go." And she left to finish dressing.

Camilla again went into the garden and cried out to sleepy Pepé, who roused himself as before and summoned the feathered fleet by calling, "Here, chickie, chickie, chickies!"

Over the hill they came, excited and eager to assist. They put their heads down and set to work: pick, pick, pick! They dropped all the Nerds onto a plate and left all the ashes. Before half an hour's time, they finished, winged each other high fives, and flapped again home.

Camilla took the plate to her stepmother, all aquiver with excitement. But Piggy, dolled up in a curve-hugging Prada column dress, shook her head and said, "Even if you *had* clothes, and even if you *could* dance, you would only put us to shame in front of everyone that matters. Sorry, sweetie, but we don't always get everything we want. I wanted a private dressing room, but did I get it?"

And with that, off went all three to the ball in a coach with oblivious Angus.

Dejected, Camilla sat down in the parlor. It was true: She had nothing to wear, and all she had in the way of moves was the Chicken Dance.

Then, all of a sudden, like a lightbulb flash over her head, she got a grand idea. Well, actually *both* of those things happened, so after she got a ladder and replaced the broken lightbulb, she went outside to the willow, looked up at the nest, and cried out: *"Bawk bawk bawk bgark!"*

Pepé the Fairy Godprawn peered down, yawning. "Oh, hello, *pollo*. *Sí*, is true, Pepé did say he would get you whatever you wish for. And a Godprawn always keep his word, okay, even if that means he never get to take the full siesta." He lowered a basket containing a gold-and-silver dress, slippers of spangled silk, and a sparkly mask. "Pepé bedazzle that mask himself," he boasted. Camilla chirped her sincere thanks, donned the garb, and rushed down the road to the feast.

At the castle, no one could place this strikingly beautiful masked stranger, not even her own family. She looked so fine in her rich clothes that they never once thought of wretched Camilla, taking it for granted that she was all alone at home in the ashes.

King Gonzo, wearing a lavender tux with matching satin bow tie, soon came up to her and said, "May I have this dance, my attractive, mysterious guest?" Beneath her feathers she blushed. This king was *handsome* with a capital AND SOME. He took her by the wing and led her to the center of the room. He was utterly charmed by her Chicken Dance. In fact, he never left her side all evening, and when anyone else asked to cut in, he said, "This fine specimen is dancing only with me." The hour soon grew late and she felt she should get home. "I'll call you a taxi," offered Gonzo, hurrying to the curb and whistling.

Camilla panicked—she had no money for cab fare!—

and she tried to slip away. The king caught sight of her in time, however, and followed secretly at a distance, hoping to find out where this beauty lived. By the time she reached her house, she was wise to her pursuer. She dashed unseen into the canopy of weeping willow branches, changed out of her beautiful clothes and into her gray frock, and sprinted inside.

Gonzo couldn't imagine how she'd managed to disappear. He politely knocked at the front door. When Angus answered, the lovesick king told him that he suspected an unknown maiden from the feast had hidden herself in the home. A thorough search turned up no one except a kitchen maid lying by the fire in her dirty frock, her head tucked under her wing. Gonzo left, deeply disappointed but no less determined to find this hottie of a hen.

On the second night of the feast, when Camilla's stepmother and sisters were once again gone, the chicken went to the willow and cried out: *"Bawk bawk bawk bgark!"* And this time the kindly but sleepy crustacean woke and lowered an even finer dress/shoe/mask combo than the one he had given her the day before, calling down, *"De nada*, okay!"

When the beautiful chicken swanned into the ball, everyone crowed—no one more so than Gonzo. They spent another splendid night together, and when the end of the ball approached and she tiptoed away, Gonzo again followed. But she was too quick and, reaching home, sprang away from him all at once into the backyard. Not knowing where to hide herself, she dove into the pool and stayed beneath a blow-up raft floating in the middle with only her beak above water till the king had gone.

The third evening, when her stepmother and sisters had left for the feast, she went again to the willow, where her kind prawn pal was already awake and waiting. He delivered a dress even finer than the former one, and slippers that were made of 24-karat gold.

They were so pretty. They were *so* heavy.

When she arrived at the feast, no one knew quite what to say: Her beauty was staggering, and thanks to her footwear, so was she. But Gonzo didn't care one whit. He Chicken Danced with nobody but her, and when she wanted to go home he said to himself, "I won't lose her this time—goodness knows, in those shoes she can't run fast or far!"

But alas, he played it wrong: When he turned to momentarily greet the members of his house band, the Electric Mayhem, Camilla ditched the shoes and skedaddled in a blink. Realizing he'd been outfoxed, the king strained to deadlift the slippers and grunted, "I will search the kingdom till I find the lady that can wear these! Then I will see the doctor about this hernia."

Word of his hunt soon made its way around town, and Piggy's ears perked up. She told her kin that this was their last chance to launch themselves into royalty, so, at all costs, they must make the shoes fit.

When the king arrived at their home, Piggy went with Andy into the bedroom to help slip on the slippers. But try as they might, they couldn't get Andy's big toes into the tiny shoes. "Never mind," said Piggy, passing Andy a knife. "Cut them off."

"What?!" exclaimed the perplexed porker.

"Go on, do it. When you're living in the castle you won't care about toes—you'll have a limo to take you wherever you want."

Having a limo sure sounded nice, so Andy did as she commanded: two hacks, and bye-bye big toes! Andy squeezed on the shoes, then limped to the king, announcing, "I win!" And since Gonzo had made a vow, they were married instantly, Vegas-style, by the limo driver/lounge singer and newly minted justice of the peace Johnny Fiama.

But, as fate would have it, on their way back to the castle, the newlyweds had to drive by the weeping willow that Camilla had planted and watered with her tears.

Through the sunroof they spotted Pepé, stretched out on a branch, strumming his guitar, and singing:

> *"Back again, back again! Check out the shoes!*
> *The shoes is too small, and not made for you!*
> *King Gonzo! Look again at that 'bride' today,*
> *Is an impostor that sit by your side, okay."*

When Gonzo examined Andy's feet, his eyes bulged even more than usual. What a gory mess! Andy, meekly trying an excuse, stammered, "N-n-new shoes always give me blisters?" The annoyed king suspected otherwise and had Johnny annul the marriage, turn the limo around, and bring the wounded impostor back home.

"Oops!" said Piggy, covering. "I made a mistake— Andy's, er, *sister* is actually the one you're meant for, King Gonzo. Let *her* put on the slippers!" And dashing into Randy's bedroom, the two pigs pushed and shoved till the shoes almost fit, save the heels. Piggy handed Randy the knife. You can probably guess what happened next.

Minutes later, Randy limped in to greet the king and said through gritted teeth, "I win!" They were married instantly, but on their way back to the castle the limo had to pass by the weeping willow, and there on a branch sat the little prawn, shaking maracas and singing:

"Back again, back again! Look to the shoes!
The shoes is too small, and not made for you!
King Gonzo! Look again at that 'bride' today,
Is an impostor that sit by your side, okay."

Gonzo looked down at Randy's feet and saw that his new spouse's white-stockinged ankles were quite soaked with blood. Randy looked at him with a little grimace and said, "Corns?" The king's face turned from blue to red. Johnny annulled the marriage, turned the limo around, and they returned.

"You sure have some desperate daughters," a perturbed Gonzo said to Angus. "Is there no one else living here who might be my true beloved and who doesn't have to do herself bodily harm to slip on a shoe?!"

"Nay, I'm effraid there ein't, me boyo," said the father, "noot unless ya mean little Camilla, the child of me first wife." The king insisted they fetch her. She bashfully entered and curtsied to Gonzo. Already bewitched by her now unmasked beauty, he set the golden slippers down on the floor before her. She stepped easily in, first one clawed foot, then the other. They fit as if they had been custom-made for her, which, indeed, they had. "Far out!" he said. "I've found my right bride!"

Piggy, Andy, and Randy, seeing how fast King Gonzo

had fallen for the chicken, knew their goose was cooked and apologized and made excuses for their hideousness, hoping Camilla would bring them to live with her in luxury at the palace. "Let she among us who is fastest throw the first stone!" proclaimed Piggy. ". . . Or something like that."

If Camilla had lips, she would have broken into a smile. The queen-to-be took great pleasure in clucking nothing at all to the terrible trio as Gonzo scooped her up and brought her to his limo. And when Johnny drove them by the weeping willow, Pepé the Fairy Godprawn sang gleefully from a branch:

"Home! home! Look at the shoes!
Princess, they make you the one he choose!
King Gonzo! Take home your bride today,
For she is the one that sit by your side, okay!"

The prawn bungeed from the branch through the sunroof, landing softly on Camilla's plush feathers. She wrapped a wing around him. Gonzo put an arm around her. Johnny cranked the radio, and off they all cruised to the castle in the most jolly of moods.

Two Brothers and a Mountain of Trouble

AFTER "SIMELI MOUNTAIN"

There were once two brothers who lived near the Rocky Mountains: Rizzo the Rat, who was decidedly wealthy, and Fozzie Bear, who was decidedly not.

Despite his good fortune, rich Rizzo gave nothing to poor Fozzie, who barely made a living as a stand-up comedian. He always kicked off his set with, "I don't mean to brag, but I possess what not a single millionaire can claim: *no money!*" He went on: "Luckily, I did sell my apartment today. I sure hope my landlord doesn't find out! Wocka wocka! But seriously, I am so hungry I was thinking about getting married just for the rice!

One day Fozzie was practicing his act while walking through the forest when, through a clearing, he was surprised to spy a large mountain he had never noticed before. While he was standing there, he heard voices approaching. In the distance, he could make out a guy in sunglasses with a ring of gray hair around a big bald spot.

Trailing behind him, incredibly, were six infant ruffians. They all carried bulky burlap sacks over their shoulders. "Hey! I know who that gang is," Fozzie whispered to himself. "It's Bobby Benson and his Baby Band, that notorious group of ruthless robbers! Which gives me an idea," he said, crafting yet another gag: "What do you call a fortune-telling kid who escapes from the police? A small medium at large!" Pleased with the effort, he patted himself on the back then ducked into a thicket, climbed a tree, and waited to see what would happen.

These six toddlers and their chaperone soon reached the base of the mountain. "All right, you terrible tykes," Bobby Benson said, "I'm not gonna tell ya again: Everything we steal goes inside this magic cavern, ya got that?" He singled out three of the wee ones in particular. "That means no keeping the silver rattle you nabbed, or that gold-plated baby bottle you grabbed, or those baby booties you ran off with."

"Aw, they killed my feet, anyway," the last said, sighing. "I shoulda known bronzed shoes weren't gonna be good for jogging."

"Point is, you little nippers, we share all the loot," Bobby said, patting his burlap sack, "so let's get this stuff stowed." Together they all faced the mountain and chanted in unison: "Mount Semsi, Mount Semsi, open up!" A doorway in the rock immediately appeared and the criminal crew entered, carrying their bags of stolen goods. As soon as they were all inside, it closed behind them.

Fozzie marveled from his branch in the tree and waited till, a little while later, the door opened again, and Bobby and his bad babies came out, sans sacks. As soon as they were all back in the daylight they chanted, "Mount Semsi, Mount Semsi, close!" Then the doorway did just that, leaving no trace of the entrance.

When they had gone, Fozzie climbed down, curious to know what they'd had in their sacks and what might be hidden in the mountain. He walked over to it and said, "Mount Semsi, Mount Semsi, open up!" and, to his delight, the mountain did as he said.

He tiptoed inside to discover a glittering cavern with heaping mounds of sparkling silver and gold, and great piles of pearls and brilliant jewels. The wheels in his brain started to spin. "Why, if I took just a little of this, I'd be so loaded, I'd need to hire a teller for my piggy bank! Ahh-AHH!" He finally decided on two handfuls of gold pieces. "Now I won't have to go hungry again—I've got what I need to make gold soup," he proclaimed, holding up a gleaming coin. "Fourteen karats! Wocka wocka!" Then he tucked it away in his pocket along with the rest.

Upon leaving he said, "Mount Semsi, Mount Semsi,

close!" And the mountain passageway closed behind him.

From that moment on, his life totally changed. He was able to eat enough to keep his stomach from hurting, he could get a brand-new whoopee cushion every time the old one popped, and best of all he was able to give freely to help anyone who was in need.

But when Fozzie had donated the last of the riches to charity, he went to his brother, Rizzo, to borrow his wheelbarrow, which he then used to secretly cart away more valuables from the criminals' mountain keep. When, later, he had given that away as well, he again borrowed the wheelbarrow from his brother.

Meanwhile, Rizzo had grown quite envious of how much the town loved his brother Fozzie for his incredible generosity. Rizzo couldn't understand where Fozzie's wealth came from, and what exactly his brother wanted with the wheelbarrow. So he devised a trap! He put a spot of glue in the bed of the wheelbarrow, and when Fozzie returned it, a gold coin was stuck to that very spot. Rizzo went to him and asked him, super casually, "Hey, bro. What have you been usin' my wheelbarrow for, anyway?"

"Just, uh, doing a little home-improvement project," said Fozzie, with a nervous laugh. "It's, er, very drafty in the living room. I mean, you can tell your house isn't properly insulated when you have to put snow tires on your vacuum cleaner!"

"Aw, stop yer fibbin' already!" The rat brandished the gold coin. "If you don't tell me the truth about where you're gettin' this treasure, I'll bring ya up on charges before Judge Judy. And you *know* she don't play."

Fearful Fozzie felt he had no choice but to tell his brother everything that had happened to him. As soon as he left, Rizzo hopped on his mountain bike and rode immediately to the place his brother had described. Once he reached the spot, he cried out, "Mount Semsi, Mount Semsi, open up!" The rock opened, he went inside and it closed behind him. There lay all the thieves' booty, and for a long time greedy Rizzo was so flabbergasted he didn't know what he should grab first. He settled on the pile of precious stones and took as many as he could carry. But as he readied to leave, his brain was too overwhelmed by the riches around him and he suddenly forgot the name of the mountain. He cried out, "Mount Simeli, Mount Simeli, open up!"

But that was the wrong name, and the mountain doorway did not budge. He tried more: "Mount . . . Sasquatch? Mount . . . Sassafras? Mount . . . Schwarzenegger?" None of them worked. He became frightened, and the longer he thought about it, the more confused he became.

Hours of attempts later—"Mount Sealy? Mount

33

Simmons? Mount Serta?"—the rock suddenly opened up, but not because Rizzo had figured out the password: Benson and his Baby Band were returning through the other side of the door.

"Youse guys!" said Rizzo, a little starstruck despite himself. "I know who you are from the news!"

Bobby said, "Why, you dirty rat. We've caught you at last."

"Caught me at last? What does that mean?"

One of the babies piped up: "Did you think we were a bunch of ninnies? That we hadn't noticed you'd already been here three times before, robbing us robbers?" He shook the silver rattle menacingly at the confused rat.

Rizzo cried out, "It wasn't me, though! It was my brother, Fozzie—honest!" Desperate, he tried to run for it but only succeeded in dashing straight into a cage Bobby pulled into his path. No matter how much Rizzo begged, and despite every excuse he gave, they didn't let him go. "You wanted to be surrounded by wealth the rest of your life?" taunted Bobby. "Well then, it's your wish come true! Enjoy the view!" And, facing the door, Bobby Benson and his Baby Band whispered too quietly for Rizzo to hear, "Mount Semsi, Mount Semsi, open up!" It did, and away they went.

But they didn't see Fozzie hidden behind a boulder

outside, and when they were gone, the charitable bear promptly rescued his brother, who was quick to see the error of his ways. Together, Fozzie and Rizzo hired a team of seven penguin miners from the nearby foothills to cart away the mountain keep's riches, which the siblings used for goodwill around the world. Said Rizzo with a twinkle in his eye when he and Fozzie received their Nobel Peace Prize, "It just goes to show ya: Getting into hot water sometimes keeps ya clean!"

Kermit the Frog-Prince

AFTER "THE FROG-PRINCE"

One fine afternoon, young princess Piggy took a walk in the forest in her bonnet, dirndl, and clogs. She carried with her a golden hacky sack, for hacking was her favorite hobby. For hours at a time she would bounce the little bean-filled bag from foot to foot. She had made an effort to play with it less, but alas, she couldn't kick the habit.

After a time, she came to a well in the woods she'd never seen before. She peered over the low row of bricks encircling it and gasped at her reflection. "A bonnet, a dirndl, and clogs?! On *moi*?!" she exclaimed, aghast. "There are literally *zero* pictures of the Swiss Miss cocoa girl on my inspiration board! *Moi*'s contract specifically said Prada would design all my outfits! Where's what's-his-name—that stage manager guy? Tell him I'm calling my agent."

So startled and distressed by her disagreeably dowdy

appearance was she that the princess accidentally dropped the hacky sack and down it fell. *Plop!* It disappeared into the inky water, which, like her appetite, seemed bottomless. She considered jumping in after it, but then she remembered that creepy girl from the movie *The Ring* and nixed that idea entirely.

Looking longingly into the well, she sang, "I'm wishing, for the one I love . . ." Then she bemoaned her loss, crying out, "If I could only get my hacky sack again, I would give everything I have in the world!" Whilst she was wailing, something swung overhead from a vine. She thought she was hallucinating till she heard a strange noise from behind her. Piggy thought it sounded like a "ribbit." She turned: The creature crouched on a low branch was not a frog, but a monkey covered in brown fur, wearing a mustard-colored vest and tie!

The primate said in the politest of voices, "Uh, hullo there. What are you crying about?"

"My golden footbag has fallen into the well and I am positively gutted." She moaned. "I mean, I'm a princess! The laws of gravity aren't supposed to apply to *moi*."

"Maybe I can help? I'm still getting used to this body but—"

"Still getting used to your body? What does that even mean?"

"Uhh, look, I'm forbidden to say more, but *if* you promise that you'll protect me, and let me visit you in your palace three times, and each time have a little food off your golden plate and a comfortable rest, well, then I can bring your hack back."

"Let you into my palace? I don't even know your name!"

"My name? Well . . . for now, you can call me Sal.

What she thought at that moment was: *Eating off my plate? Sleeping in my house? Hard pass! But . . . then again . . . my darling hacky sack . . .*

So what she said at that moment was: "Deal!"

Then, delighted, the monkey launched himself off the branch and dived deep under the water. After a little while he came up again, the footbag clutched in a dripping paw.

As soon as the overjoyed young lass had her beloved toy again, she didn't give another thought to its savior and, without looking back, hacked all the way home.

The monkey called after her, "Princess, wait! Take me with you like you said you would!" But she was already out of hearing range, the hairy helper long gone from her thoughts.

That night, just as the princess sat down to dinner, she heard that strange ribbit noise again out in the hallway.

Soon afterward there was a gentle series of taps at the door. From the other side, a familiar voice cried out:

> *"Open the door, princess dear,*
> *Open the door to the little monkey here!*
> *You must remember the promise you made*
> *By the deep well in the cool forest shade."*

The pig didn't budge. The king, her father, asked her what was the matter. "A monkey fished my hacky sack out of a well this afternoon. Wow, I think that may be the strangest sentence I've ever spoken. I told him that he could visit *moi*, thinking that he would never find the castle."

The king, who has so little to do in this story that he doesn't even get a name, told her, "If you gave him your word, you must keep it. Go and let him in." Before she could respond, the clearly irritated monkey knocked more forcefully and said:

> *"Open the door, princess dear,*
> *Open the door to the little monkey here!*
> *You must remember the promise you made—"*

"All right, furious George, I heard you the first time,"

she barked and grudgingly opened the door.

The monkey loped into the room. "Wow, you've sure got some nice digs here," he said, swinging from the chandelier. He dropped down onto the table and made himself quite comfortable between the candlesticks. He surveyed the dishes. "What are you eating, princess?"

"It's the only thing better than a talking burrito."

"What's that?"

"Adele taco!" [Editor's Note: we originally had a nachos joke in here, but it seemed too cheesy.]

When he had eaten as much as he could, the monkey said, "Sheesh, I'm getting sleepy. Please carry me upstairs?"

"Carry you? Don't push your luck, buster."

So they walked up together and the princess gave him a little pillow. He slept soundly at the foot of her bed. *Now then*, she thought when she woke to find him gone, moi *will be troubled with that nuisance no more.* But she was mistaken, for when night came she heard the same rapping at the door, and the creature who called himself Sal once more said:

> "Open the door, princess dear,
> Open the door to the little monkey here!
> You must remember the promise you made
> By the deep well in the cool forest shade."

And the pig, recalling the advice of her wise father whose name remains unknown, did open the door. The monkey came in, ate, and slept upon the pillow till the morning broke as before. And the third night he did the same.

But when the princess awoke on the following morning she was astonished to see, instead of a monkey, a handsome frog the shade of a ripe pear, standing on two scrawny legs at the foot of her bed and gazing on her with the most beautiful eyes she had ever seen.

"Hi ho! My name is Kermit. Kermit the Frog-Prince!" He took a seat, cross-legged. "It's kind of a funny story. I was enchanted by a spiteful fairy who changed me into a monkey. I was fated to live in the trees surrounding the well till a princess would agree to invite me over, and let me eat from her plate, and sleep comfortably for three nights. And you, princess," said the grateful green guy, "have broken the cruel spell. Now I have nothing more to wish for. Except maybe to never eat another banana." With that he stood to leave.

"Hold on there, buster," she said, batting her big blue eyes. "I think I should get a little something in exchange, don't you?"

"Something more than your hacky sack?"

"I'm talking marriage, Kermie. How about *toi* and

moi get hitched. Either that, or I find that fairy and tell her to change you back into a monkey!"

The frog-prince was so relieved to be free of his fur coat that you may be sure he was not long in saying yes to her proposal. In time, the princess introduced him to the addictive charms of kicking back and forth her golden footbag. And so the unlikely couple lived—and hacked—athletically ever after.

Janice! Janice!
Let Down Your Hair

AFTER "RAPUNZEL"

There was once a Las Vegas singing duo named Wayne and Wanda. Every evening, the married entertainers crooned golden oldies in a so-so casino far from the city's famed Strip, where they aspired to eventually land their act one day. But until they did, their audiences were mostly gamblers taking a time-out from losing everything except their good luck charms.

Wanda was a health-food nut with a fondness for bonnets. Earnest Wayne adored his wife and was passionate about performing, but he wasn't the brightest bulb on the marquee. One time, he played a slot machine and hit the jackpot. As the coins poured out, he told the machine, "You ought to take something for that cold." Insult to injury: The machine refused the tissue he offered.

With those winnings, though, Wayne and Wanda were able to buy a cheerful little ranch house in the desert suburbs. Out a back window they could see the house next door, an imposing castle with pointy turrets and a wooden drawbridge. (So much for neighborhood zoning laws.) It also featured a splendid garden of plump fruits and hearty vegetables protected by a tall wire fence on all sides. In an arid climate like this, such a colorful bounty would normally have been a surprising sight, but the whole block knew why this freakishly fertile plot thrived: The property belonged to the imposing Enchantress Piggy.

Like Wayne and Wanda, the enchantress also worked in a casino, performing magic. Audiences adored her act, but offstage everyone was terribly afraid of her. Her nails were long. Her patience was short. Her hair was big. Her temper was bigger.

Meanwhile, after months of waiting and hoping, Wayne and Wanda were happy to receive the news that they were soon to have a baby. One morning Wanda was standing by the window practicing her scales and gazing down into the enchantress's luscious garden when she spied the most beautiful kale. It looked so fresh, and she positively longed for it. All day she would pine away for the green leaves, and not being able to have them made her miserable and pale. Kale was her jam. She even liked kale jam.

When Wayne saw Wanda in her pitiful state, he was alarmed and asked in his smooth baritone, "What ails you, dear wife?"

"Oh, Wayne," she said, bringing the back of a hand to her forehead, "if I can't eat some of that kale from the neighboring castle's garden, I think I shall die."

Her handsome and gallant husband nodded. She was pallid without this salad, and he couldn't let her suffer. "Very well then, my dearest," he said, "I will bring you some of that kale. I will valiantly scale the fence during the night and no one will ever see me!"

"But, my darling!" She wrung her hands. "Do you feel confident your plan will work?"

"Well, only a total nut is *absolutely* positive about anything, of that I'm one hundred percent sure."

At midnight that evening, Wayne clambered over the wire fence into the garden of the lady sorcerer, hastily clutched a handful of kale leaves, and presented them to his wife upon his return. Even though it was late, she at once shredded them and dressed them and gobbled them down greedily. [Editor's Note: There was another salad joke here, but it got tossed.] The greens tasted so good to Wanda— so very good that the next day she longed for them three times as much as before. If Wayne was to have any rest, he realized he would have to sneak into the garden once again.

In the gloom of the next evening, as soon as they'd returned home from their casino gig and before he even changed out of the sparkly, faux-gem-studded white suit he wore onstage, he strode to the wire fence and scaled it. But on the other side he was surprised to look up and find the dreaded enchantress standing before him. "You thought you could sneak in here decked out in all those rhinestones without me noticing?" said the piqued pig. "You're lit up brighter than a Reno Airport landing strip!"

"Let mercy take the place of justice, my dear porcine neighbor," pleaded Wayne. "I only did it out of necessity. My wife, Wanda, who is expecting a child, saw your kale from the window and felt such a craving for it that she would have died if she had not gotten some to eat. It surely is the most impressive kale that ever sprung from the earth. Personally, I'm a terrible gardener. To wit, I can confirm that if you bury a chicken, you don't end up with an eggplant. But you do end up with a very angry chicken."

"Well," said the enchantress, her anger softened by the flattery, "I am awful proud of my gardening prowess. I was clearly born with a green thumb."

"Oh, you poor thing." Wayne sighed, patting her on the shoulder. "No wonder you wear gloves so often."

The pig suddenly hit on an idea. "Tell you what: I will let you have as much kale as you want . . . but on one condition: You must give *moi* your child when it is born."

"Hmm," said Wayne, not exactly a great negotiator, "exchange some kale leaves for a baby? Sure!" So he consented to everything, and when Wanda later popped out their little poppet, the powerful pig appeared at once, gave the child the name of Janice, and took it away with her.

The enchantress was wildly overprotective. Having had her heart irreparably broken once by a disinterested frog, the enchantress was determined to shield Janice from similar romantic pains. She shut the girl into a devilish tower made of LEGOs out in the middle of the Mojave. It had neither stairs nor a door (those darned LEGO sets are always missing pieces, can I get an amen?). Right at the top was just one small window, and when its maker wanted to visit with her daughter, she stood beneath it and brayed: "Janice! Janice! Let down your hair."

The girl had by now grown into a gangling young rocker chick with magnificent hair that had not been cut since her birth. It was almost twenty feet long! Whenever she heard the call of the enchantress below, she unfastened her tresses and dropped them down, and the pig used them to climb up.

"I, like, can't wait till they invent ropes." Janice sighed.

"And elevators," grunted the ascending enchantress.

After a year or two, it came to pass that the king's son, Link Hogthrob, was riding on horseback through the desert and happened to come near the tower. He was a dashing pig with hair the color of straw and, perched above his close-set baby blues, a pair of bushy brows to match. Link halted his horse, stood still, and turned a pointy pink ear to the sound that had seduced him. His snout quivered as he listened.

It was Janice, of course. In her solitude, she passed her time jamming on an electric guitar and letting her sweet voice carry over the desert. Smitten with the sound, Link wanted desperately to lay eyes on the singer and searched in vain for the door, but none was to be found. "Curses," he said, flummoxed. "This tower is like a plate of cauliflower: No matter how much you try, you just can't get into it." Dejected, he rode home, but he vowed to return daily.

Once when he had come to hear the magnetic voice and was standing obscured behind a wide cactus, he saw that an alluring sow had Uber'd to the tower's base. He overheard her cry, "Janice! Janice! Let down your hair." Then from the high window, tresses of glorious yellow hair cascaded, and the lady hoisted herself up.

Once the pig had climbed over the windowsill and into the tower, Janice asked, "How was work last night, Mother?"

"Not so good," the magician replied. "I'm short-staffed. I had a little accident last week while I was doing the trick where I saw my assistant in half. Now he's decided to leave the act and move to Los Angeles. And San Francisco."

Watching from outside, Link rubbed his cleft chin and thought, *If that is the ladder by which one mounts, I too will try my fortune tomorrow.* And the next day, he did indeed go to the tower. But instead of calling up to the owner of the long locks himself, for she surely would be suspicious of his deep voice, he had his sturdy steed, Buster, do the calling. The beast whinnied: "Janice! Janice! Let down your hair." Immediately the hair fell down and up Link climbed.

At first Janice was frightened to see someone other than the sorceress appear at the window. "I *thought* my mom sounded, like, a little horse," she confessed. But she was not altogether unhappy to see such a handsome hunk of pork.

The king's son was instantly smitten as well. "I am Link Hogthrob, and you are too beautiful for words. So instead I'll just make animal noises for a bit." Janice sat patiently while he worked his way through a barnyard of sounds. When he could think of no more to imitate, he asked, "Is life in this desert very terrible?"

"Well, not if you like sandwiches. And if you don't mind that instead of actual sandwiches it's just sand with more sand packed on either side of it."

"So, you don't get much rain?"

"Nope. It's like rilly rilly dry."

"How dry?"

"Last week when I mailed a letter, I had to pin the envelope shut."

Then Link, who had been trying to play it cool, could hold back his attraction to her no longer—he laid it all on the line: "My heart was so stirred by your song that it let me have no rest," said he. "Will you marry me?"

Janice was not freaked out by the question. Since he was *so* kind, and so, *so* handsome, and since living alone in the tower was so, *so*, SO boring, she said yes, and they high-fived. Then Janice realized something: "Like, how are we both going to get away from here? I can't exactly climb down my own hair, y'know?"

"Never fear—I am widely praised for my problem-solving skills," boasted Link. His brow furrowed as he thought for a moment. Then his eyes lit up. "Aha! I have arrived at a simple, practical solution: I will pilot a blimp to the window to pluck you out! I'll just need to study blimp construction. Then construct a blimp. And then take blimp-piloting lessons. Could take a couple of years."

Janice nodded with enthusiasm. "Sounds like a totally smart and practical idea."

In the meantime, they agreed that he would continue to visit in the evenings. Since the sorceress appeared in her magic gig at night, she always came to see Janice by day.

The next morning, the enchantress arrived as usual. Once she had climbed up into the tower, Janice, without thinking, remarked, "Like wow, you are so much heavier than . . ." She caught herself, but it was too late.

"Than who?!" cried the pig.

"It's actually 'than whom.'"

The sorceress was incensed. "I thought I had separated you from all the world, and yet you have been seeing suitors? *And* studying grammar?!" She huffed. "And besides, I am not fat, thank you very much. I'm just a little broad shouldered . . . around the hips." In a flash, she clutched Janice's beautiful tresses, wrapped them twice round her left hand, and suddenly held up her right hand to reveal—

"Scissors?" whimpered Janice. "Where did *those* come from?!"

The pig eyed the handle and replied, "China," then *snip, snap,* she cut off the lovely tresses.

Janice was bewildered at the sight of her hair on the floor. "Like, I don't even know what to make of this."

"One word: *extensions*. Two words: for *moi*!"

The enchantress was so cruel that she magically transported the shorn singer into the forbidding middle of Death Valley, where she had to live with no company or hope or sunscreen.

On the same day that she mercilessly cast out Janice, the pig fastened the severed hair to a hook by the window. Link innocently arrived and shouted up: "Janice! Janice! Let down your hair." When the tresses dropped, Link ascended. But instead of finding his beloved Janice, he discovered something altogether unexpected.

"Aha!" the enchantress cried mockingly, gazing at Link across the room with venomous looks, "you've come to fetch your dearest, but the beautiful bird no longer sits singing in the nest. The cat has got it, and will scratch out your eyes as well."

"Uh, hold on, I need a minute," said Link. "That's a lot of metaphor to unpack there."

"Maybe this will be clear enough: You shall never see Janice again, because you'll be trapped in this tower for the rest of your life!"

"Not true!" declared Link. "I will outsmart you, because I am widely known for my problem-solving skills!" And he leaped out the window and landed directly on a thornbush.

Buster the horse moseyed over and asked his master, "What happened?"

"Not quite sure. Just got here myself." In the end, Link somehow managed to escape without injury, if you don't count the fact that two thorns from the bush poked his eyes out and blinded him. ("Wow," he moaned, "so specific . . .") Then he wandered about the desert for years, ate nothing but roots and berries, and did nothing but lament and weep over the loss of his beloved.

Years later, he happened into the part of Death Valley where Janice wandered in wretchedness, but with a very flattering tan. He heard a voice singing, and the song seemed so familiar to him that he went toward it. When he approached, Janice was stupefied. "Like, *Link*?" She recognized her lost love and fell into his arms, weeping. Two of her tears wetted his eyes, and miraculously, his vision grew clear and suddenly he could see again. "Hey!" said Janice. "Maybe *I'm* the one with the good problem-solving skills." Link led her to his kingdom, where they married and patented Janice's restorative teardrops with a major holistic healing company.

But what of the enchantress? For her final act, to avoid the bad press about her peculiar parenting, she accepted the proposal of a certain J. P. Grosse, the king of a faraway land, and—poof!—disappeared herself from town.

Soon after, Janice reunited with her parents, the singing duo Wayne and Wanda, and together they became a critically acclaimed trio. Best of all, they finally made it to the Strip, performing at the one venue that was deliciously fitting for salad-loving Wanda: Caesars!

Not-So-Little Red Cap

AFTER "LITTLE RED-CAP"

Once upon a time, there was a bear named Fozzie who lived on a tropical island in the middle of the sea. Because of his good cheer and bad jokes, he was loved by all in the beach village (except for two crusty tribal elders, Statler and Waldorf, who delighted in heckling him). But Fozzie was absolutely adored by his grandfather, Bobo, a massive, stern brown bear who lived in a hut deep in the jungle, and who was getting on in years. In Fozzie's presence, Bobo's imposing demeanor melted, for he adored his grandson and loved whenever he came to visit.

When Fozzie was very young, Bobo had given him a little beret made of red velvet. He loved it so much he wore it everywhere. The villagers took to calling the cub "Little Red Cap." When he grew up, he still wore his beloved beret, even if it didn't quite fit his head anymore. So his nickname changed slightly.

One day Fozzie's mother, Emily Bear, said to him,

"Not-So-Little Red Cap, I've got a job for you. Your grandfather isn't feeling well, so here's a fresh-baked honey bun, his favorite. Take it to him so he can regain his strength. Go on now, before the day gets too hot, and watch where you step so that you don't trip on any roots along the way."

"You know I'm always extra careful in everything I do," Fozzie reassured her as he placed the wrapped honey bun in his backpack. "Remember when I put that safety mat in the birdbath? Wocka wocka!"

"Son, listen to Mother: Whatever you do, don't wander off the path." She hesitated, then sighed. "I guess it's time you should know something. I've kept this a secret because I didn't want to frighten you, but almost every week in the jungle a villager is killed."

Fozzie was thunderstruck. "That poor villager!"

"No, Fozzie, a *different* villager each week. They've been attacked by Spa'am, the terrible feral pig. Torn apart by his tusks and eaten! You can imagine how that must feel."

"Uhhhh, *gnawed* so good? Wocka—"

Emily's stare cut him off. "I'm serious now: Do not leave the path. And when you see Grandpa Bobo, don't forget to give him a big bear hug from me."

Fozzie nodded and set out on his way. Just as he

crossed from the bright beach into the shade of the dense tropical trees, he was met by a heavy-set pig with beady eyes and an imposing underbite. His supersize snout was flanked on both sides by fearsome tusks jutting from his lower jaw like two ivory sentinels.

"I am Spa'am," the beast grumbled.

Fozzie raised his eyebrows. "Spa'am, huh? I have a *lot* of unread e-mail messages from you!" His mother's warning had already evaporated. And besides, encountering someone he'd never met before meant only one thing to him: a new audience! "Hiya, hiya, hiya," he said, turning on the comedy razzle-dazzle. "Thanks for coming out this afternoon. I'm Fozzie Bear and welcome to my act! I tell ya, doing stand-up is hard. I mean, just look around: It's a jungle out there—literally! And I should warn you: When you're in the jungle, don't join any card games. Why, you ask? Too many cheetahs!"

The pugnacious pig didn't crack a smile.

Fozzie tilted his head. The lack of response to such stellar material puzzled him. "Hey," he said, "did you hear my last joke?"

"I sure hope so." He poked roughly at Fozzie's backpack. "What have you got in there?"

"A honey bun. My mother made it for poor, sick Grandpa Bobo, who I'm on the way to see. It'll help him get his strength back. Annnnnd speaking of strength, I woke up this morning with a real desire to exercise—so I stayed in bed till it went away!" Fozzie leaned in, peering at Spa'am up close. "Say, did you know it takes forty-three muscles to frown? Which means that right now your face is basically doing a CrossFit session."

"I'm not frowning, this is how I always look," replied the pig. "Anyway, where does this grandfather of yours live?"

"In a hut about a half mile ahead along this path, under the four largest palm trees."

"I see." The pig tapped a tusk and thought to himself, *The sooner I eat him, the sooner he will quit making jokes. What a nice plump mouthful—if I'm super crafty, maybe I can have both the young bear and the old bear!*

So after they strolled along the path for a time together, Spa'am pointed to a ripe berry patch. "I bet your poor, weak grandfather would love it if you brought him some of those," he told the bear.

"You know what you call a sad strawberry?" asked Fozzie. "A blue berry!"

The pig faked a laugh. "Why don't you hunt around and pick some for him? After all, it's such a beautiful day in the jungle. You might as well enjoy yourself."

Fozzie gazed around: The sunbeams were dancing

here and there through the foliage, and the vines swung gracefully in the breeze. So he stepped off the path and into the dense undergrowth to search. The more the bear looked, the more he found: blackberries, raspberries, and salmonberries, which he was disappointed to learn did not taste one bit like fish. Whenever he picked some, he kept spotting still riper ones farther on, and so he pressed unaware deeper and deeper into the jungle.

Meanwhile, Spa'am made a beeline to Bobo's hut and banged on the door. From inside, a deep but fatigued voice called, "Who's there?"

"It's . . . me, your, er, grandson," replied the pig. "I am bringing the, uh, bun of honey that you like. Go on now, open the door."

"Your voice doesn't sound like my grandson's. Plus he always greets me with a joke."

"Uhhhh," uttered the pig, pondering. "Knock, knock."

"Who's there?"

"Theodore."

"Theodore who?"

"Theodore wasn't open so that's why I knocked! Willy wocka!"

"Not totally Fozzie but close enough," said the bear. "I'm going to take a gamble and let you in and hope that you're not some wild pig that intends to do me harm." The latch lifted and in barged Spa'am. *Gulp!* He devoured the grandfather! Then the stuffed pig went to Bobo's bed and pulled the mosquito net that surrounded it closed. He slid into the covers and yanked them up to the jiggly skin under his chin.

Fozzie, meanwhile, had been frolicking about, blissfully picking berries, and when he had collected so many that his backpack was almost too heavy to lift, he remembered his mission and found the way back to the path.

Upon arriving at the hut, he was surprised to discover the door standing wide open. He slowly crept into the room and said to himself, "Oh dear! Something feels strange in here. Something is definitely different." Reaching the bed, it suddenly struck him: "Grandpa Bobo, you got new wallpaper!"

When the elderly bear didn't respond, Fozzie pulled aside the netting. There lay his grandfather, leering at him, utterly transformed since the last time Fozzie had seen him. "Wow," whispered Fozzie, "you must be sicker than anyone knew. I'm no medical professional, but it looks to me like apigdicitis." He leaned closer. "Oh, Grandpa, what a big snout you suddenly have!"

"The better to smell you with, my child," was the reply.

"But, Grandpa, what close-set eyes you have!" he said.

"The better to see you with, my dear."

"But, Grandpa, what hoof-like hands you have!"

"The better to hug you with."

"But for real, Grandpa—when the heck did you grow tusks?!"

"When I made up my mind to *eat you!*"

And scarcely had Spa'am said this than he sprung out of bed and swallowed Fozzie. Satisfied with his twofer treat, Spa'am lay down again, fell asleep, and began to snore very loudly.

It just so happened that soon an island cliff diver named Gonzo was passing by, and when he heard the noises from the hut he thought to himself, *Wow, Bobo's sleep apnea must be getting worse.* Concerned, he let himself inside, and when he approached the bed, he saw that it was occupied not by Bobo, but by Spa'am!

It occurred to the daredevil that the pig might have devoured the grandfather, and that he might still be saved, so he found a pair of scissors and began to cut open the villain's stomach. When Gonzo had made two snips, out jumped Grandpa Bobo.

Gonzo kept cutting until he saw a red beret, and with one snip more, out came Fozzie, who said to Bobo with a jazz-hands flourish, "Orange you glad I didn't say banana?!"

Bobo nodded, exhausted. "Yes, I really am glad. Seemed like that joke was never gonna end."

"Boy, I tell ya," said his disoriented grandson, looking around and squinting in the bright daylight, "I haven't been *that* in the dark since I gave up while taking my SATs and napped."

"Oh, I blew those tests as well," said Gonzo. "What'd you get on yours?"

"Drool!"

Bobo eyed the sleeping Spa'am. "Should we call 911?"

"We could . . . Or I have a weirder idea," said Fozzie.

Gonzo suddenly stood taller. "Weird?! Now you're speaking my language!"

Fozzie zipped open his backpack and showed them the pounds and pounds of berries inside. Gonzo nodded, and the two hoisted the bag up and dumped its contents into the sleeping pig's belly. Then they stitched him closed.

When the pig awoke, he saw Gonzo standing over him. "Doctor," yowled a grimacing Spa'am, "those bears aren't sitting so well in my stomach."

"I'm not a doctor, and those aren't bears," Gonzo said. He pointed to Fozzie and Bobo. "*These* are bears. You're filled with berries, buddy."

Spa'am blinked in disbelief. "I want a second opinion."

"Fine, I'll tell you again."

"Oh man," groaned the pig, "no wonder I have such a tummy ache—I'm very berry intolerant!" Spa'am struggled out of bed and tried to run away, but he had such a terrible reaction to the berries that he fell down dead.

Later, after his part in the vanquishing of Spa'am brought him much fame and glory, Fozzie would offer up this to anyone who asked him for advice: "Sometimes stepping off the path is actually the best thing to do. How do I know this is correct? Because whenever I'm driving down the road—*bam*! There's a sign that says 'Bear Right'—wocka wocka!"

The Pig and the Prawn Sign a Lease
AFTER "THE CAT AND THE MOUSE SET UP HOUSE"

Miss Piggy needed a roommate for her apartment in the Hollywood Hills so she put an ad in the local paper. Pepé the King Prawn answered it, and as they chatted on the living room sofa, they instantly became great friends, finding common ground in their love of Jiffy Pop, pirated cable, and mixed martial arts. "You might not know by looking at me," demurred Piggy, "but I have a black belt in karate."

Pepé raised his eyebrows, impressed. "Because you are that good?"

"Nah, because I never wash it." She took out a notebook and a pen and got down to brass tacks: "So tell *moi*: Why are you leaving your current situation?"

The prawn shrugged. "My landlord tell me he is raising the rent. I tell him that's a very good thing, okay."

"Why?"

"Because I'm having trouble raising it myself!"

She glanced at her list of questions. "Are you very particular about how an apartment is furnished?"

"Eh, not so much. Basically I just want a roof over my head. You might say I'm a ceiling fan."

"All right," said Piggy, putting down her notebook. "That ends the Q and A part of the interview. It's now time for the talent and swimsuit portion."

"Excuse me, okay?!"

"Aw, I'm just pulling your legs," she said, laughing. "You're approved, roomie!" She gave him a tour of the apartment, ending in what would be his bedroom. "Don't pay any attention to the stains on the wall," she said. "The man who lived here before was this inventor named Crazy Harry and he used the room as his lab. He mostly worked with explosives."

"Ah, so those stains are some of the stuffs that went wrong?"

"Oh, no, those are Crazy Harry."

After Pepé moved in, Piggy suggested they pool their cash and stock up on some treats to share. The prawn agreed, and off they went to the bakery, where they each chipped in equally for a half dozen assorted doughnuts. When they arrived home, Piggy blocked Pepé from going into the kitchen, whispering, "We can't take the food in there—it's infested with rats."

"Rats?! Why doan you call the exterminators, okay?"

"Oh, no, these rats are actually our next-door neighbors. They come over every morning for coffee. They're a ton of fun, but the problem is, they eat anything in sight." To keep their doughnuts from getting devoured, the two temporarily stashed the box under the couch, then went into the kitchen, where four rodents sat around the table, shooting the breeze. Piggy presented the prawn to Rizzo, Bubba, Fast Eddie, and Yolanda.

"Mucho gusto," said Pepé, using his four hands to shake all of theirs simultaneously.

"Piggy told us you were a shrimp," said Bubba, whiskers twitching, "but ya don't look so small to me."

"I am not the shrimps, *actualmente*, I am a king prawn."

"Ooo, *nobility*," said Fast Eddie, impressed. "When you get a sore throat it must be a *royal* pain in the neck!"

After they'd all had their yuks and java, the rats went back to their pad and Piggy and Pepé could safely discuss where to stash their treats. "The spot should be outside of the apartment," advised Piggy, "because the rats' sense of smell is too powerful." She snapped her fingers: "I've got it! Remember when they said that they're going on vacation this Saturday? Well, it's Wednesday now. How about we hide the doughnuts in the church across the street till they take their trip? No one would dare steal anything from there, right?"

So they went to the chapel, hid their pastries under the altar, and returned home. But before the morning was up, Piggy got an overpowering craving and said to the prawn: "Peps! I forgot to tell you! My cousin has brought a little baby piglet into the world."

"Oh? When we talk about family last night you never mention you have a cousin."

Piggy nodded slowly, buying some time to think. "He's a second cousin . . . once removed . . . from the arcade for cheating at Skee-Ball. But his little kid is soooo cute, and he wants *moi* to be the godmother. Are you all right handling the housework while I run over to the church for the christening?"

"Is no *problemo*," answered the easygoing prawn.

Of course, Piggy's story was a fib. She had no cousin with a newborn, and no one who knew the self-absorbed diva would dream of asking her to be a godmother. In actuality, Piggy went straight to the church, sneaked under the altar where the doughnuts were stowed, and ate a big bear claw. Then she took a nice nap in the sunshine and didn't return to the apartment till evening.

When she came in, Pepé had just finished Swiffering the floor. "What name did they gives the little *niño*?"

"Er . . . Bear Claw," said the pig quite coolly, fluffing her curls in the hall mirror.

"Bear Claw! That is a *muy* strange thing to call a pig, okay."

"Strange?" A small, sneaky smile lifted the corners of her mouth. "I actually found Bear Claw to be quite *sweet* . . ."

The next day, the pig felt a yearning for more and told her roommate, "Dear, dear Pepé, you'll never believe it—*moi* has been asked to be godmother to another baby!" The accommodating prawn encouraged her to go and enjoy herself. She split at once, stole into the church, and savored two fat fritters. "Nothing tastes as good as something you don't have to share," she said with relish.

When she went home, the prawn inquired, "And what did the peoples call this child?"

"Uh . . . Fritter," answered the pig.

"Fritter! Your *familia* has the very odd names, okay."

By the next day, Piggy's mouth was watering for more doughnuts. "You won't believe it, Pepé, but—"

"You've been asked to be godmother yet again," Pepé finished her sentence flatly. "*Sí*, I almost doan believe it, okay."

"Look, roomie, I know it's my turn to clean, but will you do me the favor of letting *moi* go?"

"Bear Claw and Fritter," muttered Pepé, shaking his head. "Such odd names. They make me wonder, they do."

During the pig's absence, the prawn once again cleaned the house and made everything neat and tidy. Meanwhile, Piggy was in the church polishing off three éclairs, which were the very last of the doughnuts they'd bought. On the way home, she dropped the empty box in the trash can on the street corner and blew it a kiss, saying, "Parting is such sweet sorrow."

When she got home, Pepé was seated in the kitchen, drumming his fingers on the tabletop. "Doan tell me, okay—they gives the piglet a very *loco* name?"

"Oh, I don't know. Is 'Éclair' all that *loco*?"

"'Éclair'!" cried the prawn. "With the accent and everythings? That is the *loco*-est!"

When Saturday morning finally arrived and the neighbor rats had left for their vacation, the patient prawn was more than ready to dig in to the long-anticipated doughnuts. He set out for the church with Piggy following. And yes, when they arrived, there was nothing under the altar but some crumbs.

The prawn flipped his lid. "*You!* I knew it, okay! You are no *amiga* at all! You eat all the doughnuts while pretending to be the godmother to the piggies. First you say 'Bear Claw'—"

"Ooo, just hearing that makes *moi* hungry again," uttered the pig.

"Then you say 'Fritter'—"

"I'm warning you now, Pepé, my stomach is growling—"

"Then you say—"

"I mean it, I won't be able to help myself!"

"Éclair!" was already on his lips, and scarcely had he spoken it when the hungry diva pounced, swallowed him down, and belched a most ladylike burp.

"Excusez-moi," she said, covering her mouth, "but that was one spicy prawn."

Right away, Piggy placed another ad for a roommate. The first to respond arrived the next day for a noon interview and rang the bell. She opened the door to find a squishy gray blob out in the hallway. "Hi there," it said. "I'm Chopped Liver, one of the more obscure Muppets, and I'm here about the room?"

"Chopped Liver!" Piggy's mouth began to water and she opened the door wider. "Come right in. You're just in time for lunch . . ."

Kermit and the Three Golden Nose Hairs

There was once a poor mother frog who gave birth to a little tadpole. Well, she actually gave birth to five thousand of them (frog moms are total overachievers), but one in particular was worth singling out: He came into the world with a collar around his neck—said to be a sure omen of good luck. The village fortune-teller, Madame Rhonda, predicted that in his eighteenth year this frog would marry the king's daughter, little Miss Piggy.

Soon after, King Howard Tubman—a fat boar who trumpeted his business skills, but was a big boar nonetheless—came to the village in disguise to eavesdrop on the town gossip, as he was wont to do, for he thrived on petty things. The people told him of the newborn frog with the lucky collar and Madame Rhonda's prophecy that in his eighteenth year he would marry the king's daughter.

Tubman, who was at his core very wicked, did not take this news well. He wanted no one of low birth being part of his family. The king went directly to the frog's struggling parents and, trying to mask his dark intent with charm, he said, "Your tadpole's collar means he is lucky, and, believe me, you've found your first stroke of luck." He flipped both thumbs up, then pointed them at himself: "*Me*. I'm very, very rich—I'm worth billions, frankly—and if you give him to me, I'll take care of him."

At first they refused, but when he offered them gold bricks, they changed their minds and let Tubman take their frog.

The king put the baby in a KFC bucket left over from lunch and had his driver speed him to the bank of a deep river. There, he threw the bucket into the water and thought, *I've saved my daughter from having to marry that loser amphibian. She'll thank me for this when she lands a tremendous society guy.* He got in his car, told the driver to step on it, and back home to Tubman Tower they sped.

If he had lingered, however, the coldhearted king would have seen that the bucket did not sink as he'd wanted it to do. No, not a drop of water seeped inside as it floated down the river to within two miles of the kingdom's capital, close to a mill owned by the good-natured Gonzo.

This miller was also an amateur stuntman, and at that moment, he happened to be practicing trick dives off the mill dam. "Cannonball!" he shouted as he hurled toward the water, fantasizing about the day he might be able to do such a drop from hundreds of feet in the air. When he surfaced, he saw the curious red-and-white bucket bobbing by and swam behind it till it lodged on the riverbank. He was perplexed to find inside a tiny frog with a collar. He took the foundling to his wife, Camilla the chicken, and since they had no children of their own, they believed it was a sign that they should raise him.

The loving parents named him Kermit and instilled in him, ironically, all the values the callous king lacked—among them, goodness, honesty, respect, and impeccable banjo-picking skills.

Eighteen years later, the king was weekending as usual at a miniature golf course, and as he approached the eighteenth hole, a violent thunderstorm arose. In seeking shelter, the boar happened to arrive at Gonzo and Camilla's mill—what are the chances? Since it was dinnertime, they asked him to join them. Gonzo said, "Thank goodness Camilla just happened to make rack of lamb for four tonight."

"Works for me," grunted Tubman. "And what'll the rest of you be having?"

They made do with cold oatmeal while the king snorted over his plate, pausing only to ask if the lanky frog that was so courteous to him was their son. "Yep," answered proud Gonzo. "Eighteen years ago, he floated down the river to the mill in a fried chicken to-go bucket, and I pulled him out of the water. If you get close enough he's still got a whiff of Original Recipe about him." Camilla grimaced. Gonzo went on, "Since then, we've raised and loved Kermit as our own."

Tubman realized that this Kermit was none other than the lucky frog that he had tried to do away with! Oh, how vexed he was! Without betraying his knowledge, he said, "Tell ya what, Miller, if your frog here will take a letter to my queen, I'll give him two gold pieces as a reward."

Gonzo raised his eyebrows. "Whatta ya say, Kermit? Would you be up for that?"

Kermit asked rhetorically, "Does a mayfly taste best in May?"

Tubman blinked. "I have no idea."

"Of course!" Kermit threw his arms in the air and waved them like he just didn't care.

So it was decided, and the king privately composed a letter to the queen. In it, he wrote:

As soon as the frog arrives with this letter, put him to death and bury him. Booya!

Tubman sealed the missive in an envelope and gave it, along with the gold pieces, to Kermit, who grabbed an umbrella and his banjo and immediately set off on his journey. But while keeping his head down in the driving rain, the frog got lost, and by evening he was wandering through the increasingly dark forest. Up ahead he glimpsed a single light: a cottage! He ran to it and knocked at the door. A thin guy with a mop of sea-foam-green hair and a camera around his neck opened it. He slid a pair of round-framed sunglasses down his nose for a better look at cold, wet Kermit. "You're not with the band, are you," he said, skeptical.

"No, I'm just a banjo-playing mill frog," Kermit said, "and I'm on my way to deliver this letter to the queen. But boy oh boy, am I lost. I wonder if I might be able to stay here for the night?"

"Fine by me," said the man, stepping aside to let Kermit in. "Though I should warn you that you've landed in a den of rock 'n' rollers. No doubt you've heard of the Electric Mayhem?" Kermit shook his head. "Well, I'm waiting here to get some quotes from them for my newspaper, the *Daily Scandal*, and I, Fleet Scribbler, can tell you from firsthand experience, when they come home they will be totally wired from the show and they'll insist you party with them. And partying with the Electric

Mayhem is more than most mere mortals might manage!"

But Kermit heard none of this, for he had dropped, exhausted, onto a bench and fallen immediately to sleep. Moments later, the band arrived home. "Whoa," said Zoot, the sax player, stopping in his tracks. "Does anyone else see a frog on that bench, or am I having a flashback?"

"He told me he's taking a letter to the queen," explained the journalist, "so he must be someone important."

"Hey, guys," said Janice, the lead guitarist, "should we, like, see what the letter says?"

"Definitely," said Dr. Teeth, the keyboardist. "Too bad none of us can read anything but music."

Janice nodded. "Oh, riiiiight. Bummer."

"Pass it here," said Fleet. He opened the letter and read it out loud.

After he finished, Janice was freaked. "It rilly says 'Put him to death'?!"

Fleet nodded, adding, "And it's signed 'King Tubman'!"

"Oh, dude," said Floyd Pepper as he played an ominous chord on his guitar. "He's the *worst*."

The drummer Animal erupted in echo, *"Worrrrrst!"*

"Yeah, he reminds me of a root canal I had once," said Dr. Teeth.

Lips, the trumpet player, was steamed. "I say we give this Tubman a little of his own medicine." He tore the letter into pieces and sprinkled them on the fire, then snapped his fingers a few times at Fleet. "Write this down, will ya?" He began dictating a new letter for the journalist to transcribe. "'Hey baby, when this groovy frog arrives, he and our daughter Miss Piggy should get hitched right away. Hook that up, okay? P.S.: Send out a royal decree that all miniature golf courses have to close on weekends.' There—that oughta get his goat!" They put the new letter in Kermit's envelope, then broke out the cookies and six-packs of root beer and partied till dawn. When Kermit finally woke, he pulled out his banjo, and they all jammed together on a few tunes. He thanked them for letting him crash at their place, then off he went.

Kermit reached Tubman Tower swiftly and delivered the letter to the queen—a pretty, blond-Afroed pig named Annie Sue—and to his utter surprise, the frog soon found himself both meeting and marrying her daughter, Miss Piggy, who, fortunately, had all her mother's good traits and none of her father's bad ones. Piggy likewise fell hard for the frog. As she told her mom, "Love at first sight sure saves a lot of time!"

When King Tubman came back, he was furious to learn that his wishes had been ignored and Madame Rhonda's pestiferous prophecy had been fulfilled, with the lucky frog now married to his daughter. "This is *not* what I asked for in my letter, Annie Sue. And what in tarnation does *pestiferous* mean?"

The glamorous queen raised an on-fleek eyebrow. "It means 'troublesome and annoying,' dear, which just so happens to apply to this letter, too." She handed it to him, and the king realized right away that it had been altered. "Close the miniature golf courses on weekends?! How could you *ever* have thought this was from me? Someone is trying to make me look a fool."

"Oh, they're not *trying*," Annie Sue intoned archly.

The king summoned Kermit and let him have it: "What happened to the letter I gave you, Frog, and why did you bring this other one instead?"

Kermit was dumbfounded. He glanced at Piggy, who'd rushed in behind him. "I-I-I don't know anything about it," he answered. "Someone must have swapped it while I was asleep."

"You're not getting away with this," said the king, spitting out the words. "Whoever marries my Piggy doesn't win her that easily. No, any worthy suitor must be put to the test." He thought for a moment, then his eyes lit up. "The one who marries my daughter must find the Dark, Depressing Place beyond the southern borders of the kingdom and, once there, pluck three golden hairs from the nose of the horrendous though cutely named Timmy Monster. Bring me those, and you can stay married to my daughter." By forcing the frog into sure death at the hands of this fabled beast, the king hoped to be rid of him forever.

But he didn't count on Kermit's confidence. Having grown up with the lucky collar and an ever-present optimistic attitude, the green guy simply said, "All right then, I will get you those golden hairs. Piggy is worth risking my life."

"Oh, Kermie, do be careful," cried Piggy. "I couldn't bear to be a widow!" After a moment's thought, she added, "Although I do look simply smashing in all black, so I guess it wouldn't be the *worst* thing."

With that, Kermit waved goodbye and, mounting his ten-speed bike, he began his journey. The route led him first to a large town where a watchman by the name of Lew Zealand waved him down as he reached the gates, pleading, "Wa-hey! I hope you've come with news!" Above his bushy black mustache, Lew had a nose as red as his blazer and two bulging Ping-Pong-ball eyes.

Kermit braked the bike and asked, "What kind of news are you looking for?" He always tried to be helpful.

"The fountain in the square that my fish call home used to flow with water, but now it's barely a trickle. No one knows what's wrong with it." He lifted his left hand, which held a droopy cod. "Because of that, my poor boomerang buddy is too dry to fly. It's my gimmick. Visit Yelp and you'll see all the reviews for 'Lew Zealand, the Boomerang Fish Guardsman'—that's me! But I've dropped in ranking from the number one attraction to number thirty-four, behind the miniature golf course, and that place isn't even open on weekends anymore!" Dejected, Lew flung the fish: It soared along in an unbending line, disappeared out of sight, and landed with a small though audible splat. "See? The cod's round-trips have become one way, all thanks to that blasted dry fountain."

"Gosh, I'll sure do my best to find out what's wrong with it," promised Kermit. "And I'll let you know on my way back." He peddled to the next town, where he encountered another upset gatekeeper, this one by the name of Mr. Poodlepants, a vision in a purple-and-black-checked jacket and polka-dot tie. As Mr. Poodlepants called to him, the frog put down a flipper to stop his bike.

The gatekeeper explained in a fluttery voice, stroking his beard's serpentine curls as he spoke, "A special tree in our town once bore leaves of every color in the rainbow, which I would use to make dye for these fantastic clothes I create. But over time they stopped growing and the branches are totally bare!"

"Well, just leaf it to me!" joked Kermit, but Mr. Poodlepants just peered intently at him through his red-framed spectacles. Kermit raised an eyebrow. "You're surprisingly serious, considering that outfit. But don't worry, I'll do my best to find out what's wrong with the tree and let you know on my way back."

Then he rode on until he came to a wide river, which was the kingdom's border. A wooden sign with hand-painted white letters advertised:

RIVER CROSSING: 5¢

RIDDLES: FREE

A dinghy was docked at the near shore, and on it stood a furry orange-brown bear. "Hiya!" he said, leaning on an oar. "You look like the kind of frog that has answers."

"You're apparently not alone in thinking that," said Kermit.

"Well, I sure would like to know why I always have to row people back and forth across the river, and no one ever comes to relieve me! A bear needs a break now and again. I haven't hibernated since the winter of '75." He took off his pork pie hat and wiped sweat from his brow. "Because of this darn dinghy, I've pretty much had to ditch my comedy career—although there wasn't a lot of public outcry about that."

"Gee, I'll try to find out for you," Kermit promised,

handing the ferryman five pennies. "In the meantime, can you take me to the other side? I'm in search of the Dark, Depressing Place."

"Oh, I found that a long time ago. It's the Giggle Grotto Comedy Club and it's in Van Nuys. Boy, is that room *rough*. Instead of throwing tomatoes, they throw bottles of ketchup."

"I think I might be looking for a different Dark, Depressing Place."

"Whatever you say, pal, it's your nickel." The bear shoved off. "You want your riddle now?"

"Oh, thanks, but you don't have to—"

"What's red and goes dingaling?"

"Hmm, I don't know."

"A red dingaling! I have another one: What's green and goes dingaling?"

"Well, uh, I guess a *green* dingaling?"

"Nope—they only make it in red! Wocka wocka! All righty then, here's your stop."

Now on the other side of the river, Kermit stepped out of the boat, thanked the ferryman, and after just a few minutes of walking he located the dim, smoky entrance to what had to be the Dark, Depressing Place. It was the mouth of a cave that led steeply down into the earth. When he reached the end, the passageway opened into a big, well-lit cavern. The first thing Kermit saw was the housekeeper, Yolanda, a no-nonsense rat in a flower-print housedress and apron, sitting in a tiny armchair, reading a book. Kermit glimpsed the title: *A Tail of Two Cities*. She glanced up, startled. "What the dickens!" she exclaimed. "Don't you know that a horrible monster lives here? Ain't ya scared?"

"Not really. Seems to me a lot of people who are mean or try to be scary just need a little extra kindness." Since the housekeeper didn't look so very wicked, Kermit introduced himself and went to sit next to her on the floor. "If you don't mind, I'd like to have three golden nose hairs from Timmy Monster, or else I can't keep my wife, Miss Piggy."

"We get a lot of strange types coming to our door, risking their lives tryin' to get the all-knowing Timmy to give 'em answers, but you take the cake, bub. First things first: If Timmy Monster comes home and sees ya, it'll cost ya yer life. So I'm gonna have to transform you into something small enough to hide under my chair."

"You can do that?"

She shrugged modestly. "It's a job perk. I also get Mondays off." With a deliberate blink of her eyes, the rat changed Kermit into an ant.

He marveled at his six little legs, then remembered

something. "Say, since Timmy Monster is all-knowing, would it be possible to find out three things while I'm here?"

"Sure, shoot."

"The first one is: why a fountain that once flowed freely has dried up. The second: why there are only bare branches on a tree that once sprouted multicolored leaves. And last, why the bear that rows the ferry always has to go back and forth, without ever getting any time off."

Yolanda cocked her head. "Very goofy questions," she answered, "but keep quiet and listen close to what Timmy says after I yank out the nose hairs ya need."

Just as Kermit crawled under her chair, the beast returned home, imposingly tall and plump with an all-over coating of blue-green fur. His wide mouth hung open, exposing a handful of sharp, crooked teeth. And no sooner had he entered the cave than his sensitive sniffer whiffed something. "I SMELL FROG'S FLESH," he bellowed.

"Oh pipe down. You may smell something, but it's just the fixins for tonight's celebrity goulash."

He stalked around the room, searching. Yolanda stayed put in her chair and scolded him. "I just straightened everything and now you're upsettin' it all again. Sit down and have your stew."

When he had finished eating, he immediately hit

the sack. The bed was right next to Yolanda's chair. Before long he was fast asleep, and he began to make the strangest noises. "Pay him no mind," she whispered to Kermit. "It's the celebrity goulash talking. Every time he eats a pop star he dreams he can sing. But hey—that gives me an idea . . ." The rat boldly reached up into the monster's nose and took hold of a golden hair. "Here goes nuttin'," she whispered, pulling it out and quickly dropping it under her chair next to the ant-frog.

Timmy Monster woke with a start, crying, "STRIKE A POSE!" His eyes bulged. "What do you think you're doing?!"

"I had a bad dream, so sue me." Yolanda shrugged. "I must have reached out in my sleep."

"Ooo, I love dreams," he said, suddenly intrigued. "Tell me about yours."

"I dreamed that a fountain in a town square that use'ta flow like crazy had dried up. Wonder what would cause something like that?"

"Oh, that's an easy one," answered Timmy. "My thirsty monster cousin Doglion has dug a tunnel underneath and lies there lapping up all the water before it can reach the fountain."

"Why didn't he just drink right outta the fountain?"

"Tastes fishy. If the townspeople would just get

him his own big water bowl he'd gladly come out from underground and the fountain would flow again."

When Timmy went back to sleep, Yolanda yanked the second hair out.

"What are you doing?!" cried the monster.

"My bad, my bad," she said. "I did it in a dream again."

"What have you dreamed this time?" he asked, elbows on the arm of her chair, chin resting on his two palms.

"I dreamed," she said, "that in a certain kingdom there was a tree that use'ta grow all different color leaves, but now the branches are bare. What could be the reason for somethin' like that?"

"Oh! That's easy," answered Timmy. "Those leaves are the favorite snack of my monster cousin Thog. He's eaten them all. If the townspeople would just break off a branch and plant it, another tree will grow instantly and there will be enough leaves for Thog and everyone else. Now me and my nose sure hope that's the end of your dreams tonight." He lay back down. "Sing for me?"

Yolanda rapped the Beastie Boys' "No Sleep Till Brooklyn" until he closed his eyes again. Then she took hold of the third golden hair—"Nope, that's just a booger," she said ruefully, "a giant monster's giant monster booger." After wiping her hand on her apron, she located an actual hair and pulled it out. Timmy Monster jumped up, roared, and would have eaten her if she hadn't said, "Who can help bad dreams?"

"All right, fine," he said, unable to ignore his curiosity. "What was the dream this time?"

"I dreamed of a bear on a boat who's gotta always ferry from one side to the other. How can he get a break?"

"It's simple," answered the monster. "When anyone wants to go across, the bear must put the oar in his or her hand, and then the bear will be free and whoever has taken the oar will have to ferry until they can figure out the trick for themselves. Now can I please get some zzz's without you making the inside of my nose bald?!"

Since Yolanda had plucked out the three golden hairs she promised Kermit, and since his three questions were answered, she let the monster alone, and he slept. When she turned Kermit back into frog form, he thanked her for helping him and left, content that everything had turned out so fortunately. She called after him from the cave entrance, "I'm always up for visits, ya hear? Mondays are good!"

Once the bear had ferried them back across the river, Kermit told him Timmy Monster's tip about how to get free of the dinghy.

"Ahhhhh, that totally makes sense," said the ferryman, a faraway look in his eyes. "At open-mic nights back on the comedy circuit, when audiences would yell at me, 'Please! Stop! Let someone *else* go!' I thought it was because they hated my act. But now I realize they were just saying to my future self 'Hand over the oar'!"

Kind Kermit didn't betray his doubt. "Uh, yeah, sure, that's probably what they meant."

The frog went on his way to the town wherein stood the leafless tree. He told Mr. Poodlepants what he had heard from Timmy Monster about Thog, the leaf eater: "Break off a branch and plant it, and soon there will be enough leaves for all." The watchman and the villagers were overjoyed, and to show their appreciation, they gave Kermit a donkey with a basket of gold coins on its back.

Next, he came to the town whose fountain was dry. He told Lew Zealand what Timmy Monster had said: "Doglion has burrowed underneath and he's drinking all the water. If you place a big bowl for him somewhere else, he'll leave the fountain and it'll flow again." The watchman and his town rejoiced, and they gave Kermit a second donkey with a large basket of gold coins.

At last the lucky frog reached Tubman Tower, where Miss Piggy had the Electric Mayhem crew rocking out at a ticker tape parade to welcome her hubby home. Kermit immediately took Tubman the three golden nose hairs, but the king paid them no mind when he saw the donkeys laden with precious metal: "My dear frog, tremendous job!" he said, practically salivating at the sight. "Tell me—where did those baskets of gold come from?"

"Near the south border," he said. "You just have to cross the river."

"So, if I went there I could score free gold, too?"

"Hey, it's worth a shot," cagey Kermit said, nodding. "Just ask the ferryman to take you over. He'll be *very* glad to see you."

The greedy king set out in all haste, and when he came to the river he demanded the bear take him across and wouldn't even pay the five cents. At the other shore the bear handed Tubman the oar and said, "Hold that for a sec, will ya?" The king took it and out sprang the ferryman from the boat.

"Where do you think you're going?" barked the king.

"I'm going straight to the Giggle Grotto in Van Nuys," the bear called back over his shoulder as he marched down the road. "It's comeback time!"

And from that moment on, the king has been stuck ferrying travelers back and forth. It was a punishment for his wickedness, of course, but he neither caught on nor learned a single lesson from his ordeal. Which just goes to show: You can lead a boar to water, but you can't make him think.

The Eagle, the Mouse, and the Wedge of Cheese

AFTER "THE MOUSE, THE BIRD, AND THE SAUSAGE"

Once upon on a time, an eagle, a mouse, and a wedge of cheese became pals, shared a house, and divided up their duties. Sam Eagle's work was to fly every day into the forest and bring back logs. Miss Mousey fetched water from the well, lit the fire, and set the table. And François Fromage, a stinky but suave French cheese, took on the cooking.

For a good long while, everything was just about perfect for these BFFs. "But we're never simply happy to live well if we think we can live better," said the three-headed monster Tom, Dick, and Harry, who somehow sneaked into this story then silently slipped off.

One day as Sam made his way to the woods, he bumped into Lindbergh, a kiwi-bird paramedic whom he knew from their time together in flight school, and the two sat down for lunch to catch up. Sam asked the waiter for an order of squirrel kebabs, while his friend chose the crayfish casserole. As they ate, Sam told his old pal about his enviable living situation. "I have two of the most upstanding and respectable roommates in the area—nay, in these entire majestic United States of America. Every day François greets me with a boisterous *'bonjour!'* And Miss Mousey always curtsies and says 'please' and 'thank you.' And we operate on an absolute democratic division of labor. I fly every day into the forest and gather wood. Miss Mousey brings water from the well, gets the fire going, and lays the table. And François is a *très* fabulous chef."

Lindbergh laughed. "Dunno 'bout all that, mate," was his tart response, his New Zealand accent thicker than the casserole in his bowl. "Sounds ta me like you're gettin' taken advantage of. You're doin' all the hard work while the other two just sit around at home and relax."

His friend's comments made Sam think. He scratched his flat head. He pecked another bite of squirrel and chewed slowly, trying to picture what his roommates would be doing right about now. After Miss Mousey had made her fire and carried her water, she went into her room to rest and watch *Keeping Up with the Koozebanians* until they called her to set the supper table. Why, come to think of it, she never even changed out of her pajamas, robe, and nightcap!

And sure, François stayed by the pot during the

cooking, and when it was nearly time for dinner he'd roll himself once or twice across the meat or through the vegetables so that they were flavored and ready. *But as for the rest of the day,* thought Sam, *what do either of them do?*

After his unsettling meal with Lindbergh, Sam skipped going to the forest altogether. The eagle instead flew directly home and basically blew up, venting to his roommates, "It is unjust! I have been your lackey long enough! You have made a fool of me, and that must change henceforth."

"But, Sammy," protested the cheese, "what would I do without you? I'll never find ze wingman as good as you!"

Miss Mousey wrinkled her nose and shrugged. "Why upset a good thing, Sam?"

François pressed his case. "Zis eez a *bon* situation, no? We three, together we have ze, how do you say, *je ne sais quoi?*"

The eagle eventually gave in, but he still insisted they change chores. They determined the new order through three rounds of rock, paper, scissors. The results? François would bring the wood, Miss Mousey would cook, and Sam would fetch water.

The next day, François rolled down the road to the forest, Sam went to the well, and the mouse climbed up on the stove to tend a pot of stew. But by afternoon, the Frenchman had still not returned, and Sam and Miss Mousey both feared something was amiss.

Feeling responsible, Sam volunteered to go searching, and it wasn't long till he met a mangy, ash-gray cat on the road licking her lips. "Pardon me, ma'am," said Sam, "but have you seen a wedge of cheese about yay high and yay wide?"

"Sure, honey, I done saw it, and I done ate it," replied the feline in a syrupy southern drawl. "A cat's gotta do what a cat's gotta do."

"Villain!" exclaimed Sam. "Identify yourself!"

"Oh now keep ya pants on. Name's Catgut, and it was a citizen's arrest—the thing was bookin' down the street doin' at least fifty-five in a thirty-mile-an-hour zone. I'm a hero is what I am—that cheese coulda creamed someone!" [Editor's Note: There were originally more cheese puns here, but they ultimately seemed whey too much.] Catgut continued, "Now if y'all will excuse me, mah appetizer was tasty enough, but I'm still on the hunt for mah supper. Bye now!"

Sam watched as the cat meandered off. "Oh, it's all my fault," he mourned. "Poor, pungent François. I say, when they made that cheese, they broke the mold." The bird morosely took on the cheese's task, gathering up the wood and carrying it home, where he related what he had seen and heard to Miss Mousey. They were deeply saddened but agreed to do their best and remain together.

The bird laid out the tablecloth, and the mouse made ready the pot of noodles. She wanted to flavor them, but, as she paused at the lip of the pot and pondered what good it might do for her to swim around and around in it as François used to, she lost her footing and fell in.

When Sam came to help serve dinner after collecting the twigs and logs, Miss Mousey wasn't there. In his distress to find her, he dropped the wood around the kitchen. He called and searched, but the cook was nowhere to be found. Owing to Sam's carelessness, the wood caught fire and a blaze ensued. The eagle rushed to fetch water to put it out, but the bucket dropped into the well.

This ending might have been a literal downer—because Sam, too, fell in and hasn't been heard from since—but one figure made out surprisingly well from all the mayhem: that was Catgut, who happened by the open kitchen door before the flames grew too big. She managed to pull the aromatic pot of mouse-infused noodles out into the yard, declaring, "A cat's gotta do what a cat's gotta do, y'all!" Then she savored her yummy supper and, thanks to the warm fire, which crackled all night, she enjoyed the best sleep she'd had in all of her nine lives.

Veterinarian's Hospital
Makes a House Call

AFTER "THE WOLF AND THE SEVEN LITTLE KIDS"

Once upon a time, Miss Piggy adopted seven orphan-boy piglets, and she bestowed upon them all the Golden Globe–winning love of a mother for her TV children.

One day she went to Veterinarian's Hospital, where she worked as a very glamorous nurse, while her usual babysitter, Geri, an elderly vocalist, was on tour with her all-seniors band, The Atrics. So Piggy, in her impeccably tailored pink scrubs, gathered all seven kids around her and said, "Listen to *moi*: While I'm out today, you're going to have to be on your guard against the monster Gorgon Heap. If he gets in, he will devour you and—"

The eldest interrupted. "Goodness gracious! Maybe you shouldn't say any more, lest you scare the youngest among us."

She turned to the very youngest and didn't mince words. "He will swallow you in one gulp—shanks, skin, snout, and the whole shebang. This is tough love, tots. I'm not putting you all through braces and private school only to see you get gobbled up by some goblin."

"But," the youngest tentatively asked, "how will we know if it's Gorgon Heap?"

Piggy listed the ways: "Rough voice, beach ball–shaped body. Giant purple paws with claws. Orange nose like a fat carrot. About seven feet."

"Oh my!" said the youngest. "That is an *awfully* big nose."

The eldest pig stood and vowed, "We promise to take good care of ourselves. You may go without worry and do your selfish duties at the hospital."

From the corner of her mouth, Piggy grumbled, "Do I have to tell you every single time: The line is '*selfless* duties,' not 'selfish'!"

"Selfless duties! That's what I meant. Oh please, Miss Piggy, don't dock my allowance again."

"We'll discuss it later," said Piggy, "when the reader isn't around." She patted each of them on the head, and left for her shift.

It was not long before someone rang the doorbell and called out in a suspiciously gruff voice, "Open up, my tiny tenderloins. It's your mother, Miss Piggy, and I have missed you so very much."

"We will not open the door," cried the eldest, "because you aren't our mother. Piggy would never be that cloyingly sentimental, and also she has a soft, pleasant voice that she describes as a 'Carly Rae Jepsen pop mix crossed with a Patti LuPone Broadway belt.' But your voice is rough. You sound like a cross between Al Pacino and a cement mixer. We're not fooled: You are Gorgon Heap!"

Thwarted, the crafty monster shambled to a bakery and appealed to the terrified proprietor, Beaker, whose shock of hair stood on end like a fluffy orange crown.

"Gimme some sugar," growled Gorgon, pounding a purple fist on the countertop.

Beaker meekly squeaked, *"Meep meep meep?"* And he held out his thin, lab-coat-clad arms wide and hugged Gorgon Heap.

"Not *that* kind of sugar," spat the creature, stepping back from the baker's grasp. "I want some *real* sugar. I'm going to eat it to make my voice softer and sweeter. About a cup will do."

Beaker poured out one cup of sugar with quivering hands, losing about two cups on the floor in the process. Gorgon grabbed the sugar, gobbled it up along with the measuring cup, then returned to the pigs' house. He rang the doorbell and cried, "Open up, you succulent cutlets, your mommy is here and she has brought a gift back with her for each of you."

But while Gorgon's voice was indeed sweeter, the eldest still didn't buy it. "Piggy only gets *herself* gifts," he said, noticing that Gorgon had unknowingly pressed his paws against the door's frosted window. "Also, Piggy doesn't have purple fur! We will not open the door— you're Gorgon Heap!"

Foiled again, the crafty monster hurried back to the bakery. Beaker fumbled for the sack of sugar and held it up. *"Meep?"*

"Not that," said the monster.

With an inquisitive look, Beaker held out his arms. *"Meep meep?"*

"*Definitely* not that. I need you to sprinkle some flour on my paws so they don't look purple." The baker did as he was commanded. Gorgon held them up for inspection. Satisfied, he clapped Beaker on either side of his head in thanks, leaving him dazed and dusted in a cloud of flour.

So now Gorgon Heap went for the third time to the pigs' house, rang the doorbell, and said, "Open up for me, my little bacon bits, your dear mom has come home, and has brought every one of you something back from the bakery with her."

The little pigs cried, "First show us your hands so that

we may know if you are our dear Piggy." Then Gorgon put his paws against the window, and when the pigs saw through the frosted glass that they appeared to be pale like their mother's, they believed that all they heard was true and opened the door.

As the monster galumphed inside, the eldest shouted, "Gorgon Heap has breached the hull! It's every pig for himself!" The horrified hogs hurried to hide. One sprang under the table, the second into the bed, the third into the stove, the fourth into the kitchen, the fifth into the cupboard, the sixth under the sink, and the seventh into the grandfather clock case.

But Gorgon Heap found them, and one after the other he swallowed them whole, right down his throat. The youngest, who was in the clock case, was the only one he didn't discover. When the monster had satisfied his appetite, he walked a short distance, laid himself down under a tree in the green meadow, and fell asleep.

Soon afterward Piggy came home from work, and what a sight she saw! The table, chairs, and lamps were overturned, the sink lay broken in pieces, and the quilts and pillows were pulled off the bed. When she saw none of the piglets, she called the ancient call that usually brought them running: "Soooeeeee! *Soooooeeeee!*" But they were nowhere to be found—until the grandfather clock chimed six times and the youngest staggered out holding his ears. The wee one told her through tears that Gorgon Heap had eaten all the others. Piggy was steamed. "If that monster thinks he can take on *moi*, he's got another think coming."

She marched out the front door, the piglet trailing her. When they came to the meadow, there lay the creature, more plumped-up than ever. Piggy examined him—right away she saw that something was moving and struggling in his engorged belly. "Holy *chicharrones*," she blurted, then told the youngest, "run along to Veterinarian's Hospital and fetch Dr. Bob and Nurse Janice!"

Soon he returned with the medical professionals and Piggy relayed the patient's history to them while they put on their gloves and prepared tools for the operation. Meanwhile, the youngest piglet tapped the doctor's elbow. "May I ask you a question, Dr. Bob? I have a ringing in my ears. What should I do?"

"Don't answer it!" replied Dr. Bob. "If it's really important, they'll text."

Just then, Nurse Piggy noticed Janice had her right and left shoes mixed up. She told her, "I think your sneakers are on the wrong feet."

"Nah," said Janice, shaking her head, "I'm, like, pretty sure these are my feet."

"But," Piggy continued, bending down to look closer at the shoes, "today isn't Friday—why'd you write TGIF on them?"

The blond nurse swept her hair out of her face. "Oh, that stands for 'toes go in first.'"

Just then, Dr. Bob took his scalpel and made a cut on the sleeping monster's stomach.

"Uh-oh," said Janice, who was holding its wrist. "His blood pressure is rilly low."

The dog chortled. "Wait'll I give him my bill—that'll raise it!" He made another cut, and one of the little piggies thrust its head out! When Dr. Bob cut farther, all six sprang from its gut, one after another, still alive.

They embraced their dear mother, and she pondered, "What should we fill his belly with? They already did the berry trick in an earlier story."

The eldest held up a hoof: "I know! I'll go to Party Universe and buy a big helium balloon."

"Perfect," Piggy told him, "and we'll fill the sleeping beast's stomach with it."

"While we wait, Dr. Bob," said Janice, "I've been meaning to ask you for some medical advice: Every morning after I pour my coffee into my mug and drink it, I get a stabbing sensation in my eye."

Dr. Bob had an immediate diagnosis: "Why don't

you try taking out the spoon!"

The eldest soon returned with the balloon, and Dr. Bob stuffed it into Gorgon Heap's stomach. They sewed him up again right away, then hid behind a tree to wait for him to wake.

"Hey, Mother," said one of the sons, half lost in thought, "how come 'fat chance' and 'slim chance' mean the same thing? And also: *hedgehogs*. Why can't they just *share* the hedge?"

Piggy sighed. "I should have known what would happen when I named you Non Sequitur."

The monster finally roused. He was very thirsty and wanted to go to the pond to drink. But when he began to walk, the helium inside him lifted him off the ground. Everyone cheered as he sailed up, up, and away!

And so we come to the end of another episode of Veterinarian's Hospital. Tune in next week, when you'll hear Dr. Bob say, "Did you hear about the guy who lost his whole left side? He's all right now!"

Hungry Rowlf and the Big-Hearted Bird

AFTER "THE DOG AND THE SPARROW"

Rowlf, a nut-brown mutt of indeterminate age, had a thoughtless master who took terrible care of him and often let him suffer the greatest hunger. After a while, the downtrodden dog could bear the ill treatment no longer—he took to his heels with a gruff *"ruff,"* and off he ran in a very sad and sorrowful mood.

When he reached the road, he met a downy white chicken. The friendly chick, who introduced herself to him as Camilla, suggested that he come with her to the next town, where she promised to find him plenty of food. When they arrived, she took him immediately to the Swedish Chef's Butcher Shop. When no one was looking, she used her wings to flap herself up and perch upon the countertop. She could hear the Swedish Chef in the back room, happily talking to himself: *"Børk, børk!* Charpeen dur knifen . . . *Børk, børk!* Kutten dur meats . . ."* And on he went.

When she felt certain he wouldn't come their way, Camilla pecked and scratched at a cut of meat that lay near the counter edge till at last down it fell to the floor. The famished pup downed it. "My kind, feathered friend, that was scrumptious," he said, licking his chops clean.

She asked if he would like anything else. "I sure wouldn't mind having a piece of bread," he said hopefully. "Some people aren't into carbs, but I say, hey, why go against the grain?"

With a wave of her wing, Camilla indicated that he should follow. She led him along the street to Beauregard's Baked Goods. There, she pecked at a baguette displayed in the open window till it fell right into Rowlf's outstretched paw. When the dog finished it off and still wished for more, she took him to Dr. Honeydew's Fruit Stand and pecked down some blueberries for him.

Camilla had delivered him a veritable pupu platter of purloined bites, and the dog was in hog heaven. "I think a little exercise might do me good now," he said, rubbing his full belly. Camilla suggested a dip in the ocean, but Rowlf balked. "I hear swimming keeps you fit, but come on—have ya ever seen a whale? I think a nice simple walk might be the ticket."

They strolled along the high road till Rowlf said he was too tuckered out to continue. "My stomach is not used to working this hard! I think maybe I'd better take a little nap right here." The groggy doggie laid himself on the cozy warm dirt and fell fast asleep. Likewise, Camilla settled herself for a snooze in the shade of a sycamore just off the lane.

Whilst they slept, there happened by the demented local veterinarian, Dr. Phil Van Neuter, and his hulking wife, Composta Heap, riding in a cart drawn by three horses. Phil had a feathery fluff of gray hair plopped atop his oblong face, a nose like a corn dog, and lamblike ears that stuck straight out on either side. He always wore oversize brown gloves on his disproportionately enormous hands, making him look more like a welder than a doctor.

Composta, his blue-hued honey, had looks so challenging, at home they had to put shatterproof glass in their mirrors. In the garden, she could pick the corn and be the scarecrow at the same time. Her three chins clumped together like a trio of plump plums fighting for space on her chunky neck, and beneath her eyes were bags so heavy they practically each required a bellman. Her limp, acid-yellow hair was gathered into a ponytail that pointed up at the sky, which gave her huge head an unfortunate pineapple silhouette. Indeed, a look at her felt like a tropical punch.

The duo was returning from their local coffee shop, Fantastic Beans and Where to Find Them. The wagon they rode in was loaded with two casks of nitro cold brew. The java junkies were inordinately fond of caffeine, which was the second reason why the animals in town were less than excited if they happened to find themselves on shaky-handed Dr. Van Neuter's operating table (the first reason? Just look at his name).

The chicken was roused from her sleep by the sound of the approaching cart's wheels. She opened her lids in time to see that Phil and Composta were on a direct course for her sleeping pal Rowlf and would almost certainly run him over! She immediately cried fowl, blurting out a series of distressed squawks to the driver.

Phil heard her but dismissively raised a brown glove, waving her off. "I'm a busy man, bird. I don't have time to slow down and talk with you. Make an appointment at my office." Although he always sported a pair of spectacles secured with a strap around his head, his eyesight was questionable at best, and he couldn't see that Rowlf lay directly in the path of his cart.

Camilla said that he would be sorry if he didn't stop immediately, but the doc only sneered at her warnings. Then, in a very dark, deeply disturbing twist that animal rights activists will probably picket, he drove the cart right over poor Rowlf! True, cats may have nine lives, but math was not in this dog's favor—it was curtains for the canine.

"Bgarrrrrrrrrrk," wailed Camilla.

Careless Phil merely scoffed at her outburst. Without even looking back, he called over his shoulder, "It was a pothole we hit, nothing but a bump in the road." And they continued on their way.

But the aggrieved chicken, vowing vengeance, caught up with the cart and, unseen, crept under it. She pecked at the cork of one of the casks till she loosened it, letting all the coffee dribble out without either Phil or Composta knowing.

It wasn't until much later in their journey, which Camilla stealthily tracked from the shadows of roadside trees, that Phil finally noticed the cart was dripping and the cask was quite empty. "I'll be darned! What rotten luck. Half our nitro cold brew is spilled!"

But Camilla wasn't finished with these dastardly dog squishers. She alighted upon the back of one of the horses and pecked at his head till he reared up and kicked. When Phil spied what was happening, he drew out a hatchet and aimed at the chicken, but she flew away just in time and the blow fell instead upon the poor horse's head with such force that it fell down dead. "I'll be darned!" cried he. "What rotten luck. Half our nitro cold brew is spilled, and now one of our horses is dead!"

The chicken crowed in triumph, but she wasn't done yet. As Phil and Composta boarded their cart and, led by the remaining two horses, tried to hurry away from further peril, Camilla again crept under and pecked out the cork of the second cask so that all the coffee ran out.

When Phil discovered this, he again cried out in despair, "I'll be darned! What rotten luck. One of our horses is dead, and now *all* our nitro cold brew is spilled!"

Meanwhile, Camilla had perched on the head of the second horse, and pecked at him, too. Phil flailed at her again with his hatchet, but away she flew just in time, and the blow instead fell upon the second horse and killed it on the spot. Camilla then perched upon the third horse and began to peck him, too. Phil was by now livid, and without looking around him or caring what he might hit, he struck again at the chicken—and killed his third horse. "I'll be darned!" cried he. "What rotten luck. All our nitro cold brew is spilled, and now all our horses are dead!"

Camilla skedaddled on ahead of the careless couple and ducked out of sight. Without horses to pull the cart, Phil and Composta were forced to leave it behind and hoof it home, overflowing with rage. It was a long and exhausting walk, and when they finally reached their house, they saw that the front door stood wide open.

They went warily inside and minutes later, the doctor heard a scream from the kitchen. He dashed into the room and saw Composta standing among dozens of rowdy rats who were scurrying around the pantry and open fridge, eating food from smashed containers and torn-open packages. "I'll be darned!" cried he. "What rotten luck. All our nitro cold brew is spilled, all our horses are dead, and now all our food is eaten!"

"Hey there, Van Neuter," said one of the rats. "Rizzo here. Ya might not remember us from your testing lab."

"You!" Phil was surprised to see him. "I thought you'd been stolen!"

"Nope. I picked the lock. And these are the pals I sprung along with me. They're not too happy witcha, either."

Camilla sat on the windowsill and clucked in delight at Phil's consternation. He spotted her and figured that she was behind this latest injustice, too. He jumped up in a rage, seized his hatchet, and chucked it at the chicken. But he missed and only managed to shatter the window. Camilla flapped over to the wooden dining table and perched upon it, wiggling her tail feathers and taunting him with a drawn-out, *"Baaaaawwwwwwkkkkkkk!"*

Frenzied Phil retrieved the ax, eyed his target, and struck the table with such force that he cleaved it in two without touching Camilla. As the chicken flapped from place to place and rats scurried for cover, Phil and Composta were so furious in giving chase that they broke all their furniture, glasses, chairs, benches, and even the walls. Finally, the chicken plopped herself atop the doctor's head. He stood stock-still as Composta, now holding the hatchet, edged closer and suddenly swung—but fleet-footed Camilla was quicker and darted away just in time. Phil's noggin took the brunt of the blow and down he fell.

Composta shook her pineapple head, dazed amid all the destruction. "What rotten luck," she wailed. "All our nitro cold brew is spilled, all our horses are dead, all our food is eaten, all our furniture is smashed, and now my Phil's a goner. But there *is* some good news . . ." And here she made goo-goo eyes at Rizzo. "That means I'm single again!"

And that was the day the Guinness Book clocked the world record for the four-hundred-meter dash, set by Rizzo, who still hasn't stopped sprinting.

Fozzie's Super-Sticky Situation

AFTER "THE GOLDEN GOOSE"

Mildred Huxtetter was mother to three very different boys. On this day, her eldest son, Seymour, an elephant, wanted to go into the forest to chop some wood, so before he went, Mildred gave him a brown paper sack that held a delicious cupcake and a bottle of juice.

Not long after Seymour entered the trees, he encountered a little orange figure with long, skinny limbs and a mane of fuchsia hair who was drumming on some red-capped mushrooms with twigs. "Animal!!!!" the figure shouted when he saw the elephant. "Animal hungrrrrry! Thirrrrsty!"

Seymour stepped back, guarding his lunch bag and flapping his ears in irritation. "Are you one of those fairy-tale dwarfs?"

"NOOOO! I . . . am . . . Animal!" came the reply.

"Your name is *Animal*?" said Seymour, looking down his trunk at the stranger. "Well, first off," he continued, "what kind of name is 'Animal'? I mean, I'm an *actual* animal and my name is not 'Elephant.' I'm sure you agree that's weird. And second, if I give you my cupcake and juice, I won't have any for myself. Sooooo, it's going to be a no from me." And he went on his way.

But Animal had his payback later when Seymour began to chop down a tree. The callous fellow swung the ax and completely missed the trunk—but he *did* hit his *own* trunk! The pachyderm panicked and stampeded home in a supersize snit.

Despite Seymour's accident, the second son, Quongo, a gargantuan gorilla, decided he would go into the forest to chop the wood. Mildred Huxtetter gave him: (1) a brown paper sack that held a cupcake and a bottle of juice, and (2) a warning not to hack off any of his body parts. As he walked into the trees, he saw Animal standing before him on the path, pointing at his open mouth: "Caaaaaake! Juuuuuuice!!" Quongo ignored the peculiar beggar but after only a few blows of the ax on his first tree, he struck himself in the leg. Thank goodness Lindbergh the paramedic kiwi-bird happened to glance down while on a flyover. He airlifted the ape out of the woods and to the nearby Veterinarian's Hospital.

Back at home, the youngest son, a bear named Fozzie, rubbed his hands together in anticipation. "My turn, Mom! Can I go and cut wood now, can I? Can I?"

Mildred Huxtetter pursed her lips and looked at her youngest dubiously. "Cut wood? Have you forgotten that time you tried to be a tree surgeon and fainted at the sight of sap? Your brothers have hurt themselves at it, and *they've* got brain cells," she said, patting him on the head. "I'm not about to let you run around willy-nilly with an ax!"

Fozzie wasn't going to give up. "I'm just asking for a chance. Let me show you!" He took up the ax and in impressive time managed to chop down a tree in the yard.

His mother raised her eyebrows. "Where did you learn to cut trees like that?"

"The Sahara Forest."

"You mean the Sahara Desert?"

"Sure, that's what they call it *now*!"

She relented and gave him her permission, but the only snacks she had left for his journey were a dry biscuit and a plastic bottle of water. He didn't care. He was so excited. "Hey, Ma," he called back as he headed for the door. "What month do trees hate the most?"

"I don't know, Fozzie, what month do trees hate the most?"

"Sep-*tiiiiiiimber*!"

Mildred chuckled despite herself and shooed him out.

Almost as soon as he entered the forest, there stood

Animal in front of him, arms outstretched. *"Caaaaaake! Juuuuuuice!* An-i-mal *huuuungry. Thiiiiiirsty."*

Fozzie shook Animal's hand. "I have nothing fancy to offer you, desperate little guy, but I do have a dry biscuit and water. Come on, let's sit down and eat together."

Fozzie gave Animal the lion's share of the biscuit and the water. When the bear took a bite, he was surprised to taste not a biscuit but a fine sweet cupcake, and when he sipped from the bottle, he tasted not water but the most delicious cherry juice. By the time they finished, Animal had pepped up. He pointed at Fozzie's chest and said in his guttural voice, "Good heart. An-i-mal re-pay." He pointed to an old tree nearby. [Editor's Note: It was a dogwood. You could tell by its bark.] "Chop," Animal told him. *"Choppppppp!"* Then he scampered away and disappeared.

Fozzie followed Animal's instruction and cut down the tree. When it fell, an owl with feathers of pure gold popped out of the split trunk.

"Whoooo," cooed the owl, swiveling its head first left, then right, looking quite confused. Fozzie lifted her up, put her under his arm, and set out for home. But he only succeeded in getting very lost. Finally, after the sun had set and hope of finding the right path had faded, he happened upon an inn where he thought he would stay the night.

Now the owner of the inn was an honorable old Frackle with three not-as-honorable Frackle children named Snively, Boppity, and Gloat. These birdlike beasts saw the golden owl and immediately wanted to steal one of its valuable gilded feathers. Snively, who was olive green with a long snout and two golf-ball-size eyes, thought, *I'll find a way to pull one out!* And as soon as Fozzie had fallen asleep in his room, Snively slipped in and seized the bird by the wing. But, remarkably, her hand remained stuck to the feathers. Try as she might, she couldn't pull it away.

Boppity, who was blue with bat ears and a petite beak, came soon afterward, thinking only of how he might get a feather for himself. But once in Fozzie's room, he lightly brushed by his sister when passing and suddenly found himself firmly stuck to her.

At last Gloat, seaweed green with two fangs poking down from a row of top teeth, stole into the room with the same intent as his siblings. The others warned him, hissing, "Keep away! For goodness sake, keep away!" But Gloat did not understand why he should be excluded and thought it was a trick by the other two so they could hog all the feathers. Gloat hurried forward to grab the bird, but as soon as he bumped against his brother, he remained stuck to him. So all three of them had to spend the night glued to the owl and each other while Fozzie slept soundly.

The next morning the bear woke, took the owl under his arm, and set out for home, the directions to which the innkeeper had kindly Google-mapped for him the previous evening. Fozzie was too focused on the route to pay any mind to the silly Frackles who trailed after him.

From a distance, the local politician Sam Eagle saw the procession way off in the middle of a field (he was, after all, eagle-eyed). He hollered, "For shame, you good-for-nothing Frackles! Why are you harassing this young bear? And on election day, no less! Have you no sense of propriety and patriotism?!" He quickly caught up to them and seized the last by the hand to pull him away, but as soon as he touched him, he likewise stuck, and was himself obliged to run behind the growing line of followers.

Before long Sam's intern, Scooter, realized the politician was missing and went searching. He finally located the eagle running behind three Frackles and was astonished. "Uh, sir? Where are you running so quickly?" he called. "Is this part of the campaign? Don't forget that we have a vote today!" And sprinting along behind them, he reached out for Sam's blue tail feathers. Oh boy: bad idea.

Whilst the five were trotting thus, one behind the other, they came upon the Prairie Dog Glee Club practicing in a field. The politician called out to them and reminded them to vote, and also implored them to please help set him and Scooter free. But the seven prairie dogs had scarcely touched the eagle when they were held fast, and now there were twelve in total running behind Fozzie and the owl.

Soon afterward they came to a city where there was a ruler whose daughter, a blond beauty with a pointy snout named Afghan Hound, was deadly serious. No one had ever been able to make her laugh, not even the absurd appearance of her father, the ruler of the kingdom, who was an actual foot-long wooden ruler. So the ruler introduced a measure. He declared that whosoever was able to crack her up could take her paw in marriage.

"A comedy contest?!" said Fozzie upon hearing the news. "Now you're talking my language!" He detoured with his golden owl (and all who were attached) to appear before the ruler's daughter.

It wasn't a very auspicious beginning: Afghan Hound didn't even look up from her sudoku as Fozzie cleared his throat nervously and asked, "What do you call a grizzly with no teeth?" She ignored him, but still he gave the answer: "A gummy bear!" And he waited hopefully for her positive response. Purely by chance, she did glance up, and she saw the gleaming owl sitting on Fozzie's right hand, and the trail of twelve creatures attached to the bird, one behind the other, and she began to convulse with laughter at the preposterous sight.

Thereupon Fozzie asked to have her for his wife, but her prejudiced father was not sold on this potential son-in-law. The ruler felt if you gave a bear an inch, he'd take a mile. So he made all manner of excuses and said Fozzie must first produce someone who could drink a cellarful of root beer. The bear immediately thought of the drummer in the forest—certainly as thirsty as Animal always was, he might be the solution. So Fozzie put down the owl and rushed back into the woods alone. In the same place where the felled tree had hatched the golden bird, he saw Animal sitting with a sorrowful face. Fozzie asked him what he was taking to heart so sorely, and he answered: *"Thirrrrrrsty!"* So Fozzie led him into the ruler's cellar full of root beer barrels, and Animal drank and drank. Before the day was out he had emptied them all.

When Fozzie asked the ruler once more for Afghan Hound's paw, the fickle father added a new condition: Fozzie must first find someone who could eat a whole mountain of bread. The bear didn't have to contemplate long—he turned again to Animal, who chowed down, and by the end of one day the whole mountain had vanished into his belly.

Then Fozzie for the third time asked for Afghan Hound to be his bride, but the ruler again sought a way out, and said the bear could only marry her if he could bring him "what went up when rain came down."

Stumped, Fozzie reflected on the riddle while he walked in the forest and he soon came across the loopy little drummer. When Fozzie repeated the brain teaser, Animal just grinned. Above them in the sky—just like *that*!—the clouds gathered and rain began to fall. Animal reached behind a tree, and what do you think he grabbed? Why, he grabbed an umbrella! Because an umbrella goes up when rain comes down.

The bear returned to the kingdom and presented the ruler with the umbrella. The ruler realized that he could no longer keep the ursine suitor from marrying his daughter, so their union was immediately celebrated, with Animal as the ring bearer.

And after the ruler fell from power and was recycled, guess who inherited his kingdom?

"Who?" said the golden owl.

"Yeah, who?" echoed the twelve souls still stuck to its feathers.

"Me!" said Fozzie. And he and Afghan Hound lived and laughed happily ever after.

Snowdrop and the Seven Penguins

AFTER "SNOWDROP"

It was the middle of winter, when broad flakes of snow were falling like confetti at New Year's Rockin' Eve, that the queen of a country sat by a castle window embroidering a throw pillow. With one final pass of the needle and thread, it was done: the phrase HANG IN THERE emblazoned above a kitten dangling from a tree branch, all in cross-stitch.

Her project complete, the royal lady had pushed open the two panes of a window framed in fine yellow birch wood and accidentally pricked her finger with the needle she still held. "Hasenpfeffer!" she exclaimed at the sting as three drops of blood fell onto the fresh white snow outside. An artist by nature, the queen was immediately infatuated by the color scheme before her and mused thoughtfully, "Would that I could someday have a daughter as pale as that snow, as red as that blood, and as yellow as this window frame."

Her wish, as they sometimes do, came true: She soon

gave birth to a daughter, whom she named Janice, and who really did grow up to have skin as pale as snow, lips as scarlet as blood, and hair as blond as birch wood. Her mother affectionately nicknamed her Snowdrop. But as is the case with most queens introduced in the opening paragraphs of fairy tales, this one grew ill and, despite the positive encouragement of her pillow's message, she did not hang in there for long.

Her husband, King J. P. Grosse, eventually took another wife, an enchantress and former Vegas magician who was very beautiful but also so vain and arrogant that she could not bear to think that anyone was more fetching than she. This new wife's name was—

"Oh, waaaaait, let me guess," said Miss Piggy as she entered her new bedroom and watched the palace servants lugging in her countless steamer trunks, suitcases, and hat boxes. "It's *moi*, isn't it. I'm the evil queen yet again. Why am I always playing the villain in these stories? I'm nice! I'm *very* nice!" She turned to a servant. "Tell them how nice I am, Stephen!"

The exhausted young guy took off his round-framed glasses and wiped sweat from his brow. "Uh, my name is Scooter."

"See?" said Piggy. "How *nice* of *moi* to remember that your name started with an *S*."

Though her self-absorption was widely known, this porcine powerhouse did have secrets. Her biggest was the story behind a large looking glass that she had the court carpenter hang in her boudoir. It was charmed, and it contained the souls of two old gentlemen named Statler and Waldorf, captured as punishment for once joking about Piggy's Broadway aspirations. "She'd definitely put the 'ham' in *Hamilton*," Statler had cracked. Waldorf replied, "I think she's perfect for *Swine-y Todd*!"

But now the gentlemen always behaved when Piggy would gaze upon herself in that mirror and ask:

> *"Tell me, old coots, tell me true!*
> *Of all the ladies in the land,*
> *Who is fairest? Spill it: WHO?"*

And the imprisoned hecklers in the glass, compelled by sorcery to speak the truth, had always answered: "Your Majesty, you are the fairest of all." Which pleased her to no end.

Meanwhile, Piggy's stepdaughter, Snowdrop, was proving to be a musical prodigy. By the time she was seventeen years old she could positively shred a six-string. But her looks were even more beautiful than her guitar playing: long spaghetti-straight blond locks, plump red lips, and eyelashes as long as a daddy longlegs's long legs.

The queen was not pleased—"Understatement alert," interjected Piggy as she marched into her dressing room to quiz the mirror. Statler and Waldorf did indeed deliver the blow she feared was coming:

> *"Your majesty, you are no eyesore, it's true,*
> *But Snowdrop is a heckuva lot more fetching than you."*

"That's #FakeNews!" blurted Piggy, her pink face turning red with rage and envy. But they didn't relent, so she called on a servant to remedy the problem. In a furious voice, she said, "Stephen, take that girl away into the woods so that I never have to see her or hear about her again."

Scooter swallowed hard. "Uh, do I have a choice?"

"Sure," said Piggy nonchalantly. "Totally your choice: You can do as I say, or you can *meet the executioner*!"

"The executioner? Cool! That's Sweetums. He's actually a great guy. I'll choose that."

"Oh good grief. Just do as I say, unless you want to wind up stuck in a mirror."

"Trust us," said Statler. "You *don't* want that. It's so small in here, if we dropped a tissue we'd have wall-to-wall carpeting." But only Piggy could see or hear them, so the quip went unacknowledged.

Off Scooter hustled to slip on his lucky green satin bomber with yellow trim, which he always wore when he needed confidence. Then he led naive Snowdrop and her guitar away from the castle, but his heart melted when he had to tell her why they were suddenly out in the middle of nowhere, deep in the trees. He cleared his throat, and blurted, "I'm really sorry, but I've been ordered to do away with you!"

She took in his grave words, gathered her thoughts for several long minutes, then methodically laid out her full argument: "Like, maybe *don't*?"

"Ah jeez, Snowdrop, the honest truth is I couldn't live with myself if I did. Here." He handed her a sack. "I packed you Lunchables and a ginger ale, plus a juicy kumquat for later."

"Oh, far out! I can't resist kumquats! Seriously, show me a kumquat and I like totally gotta eat it," she said, foreshadowing heartily. "Thanks a ton," she said, taking the sack and patting Scooter on the shoulder. "You're a real pal, dude."

He left her by herself and returned to the castle. Though he thought it most likely that the wild beasts of the forest would tear her to pieces like a puppet made of felt and yarn, he hoped with all his heart that instead someone would find her and take care of her.

Seemingly doomed, Snowdrop ate her snack, then wandered along through the trees, strumming folk songs on her guitar till dusk, when she came to a quaint cottage set among the foothills. She let herself in to rest, for her cork wedges would carry her no farther.

Inside, everything was neat and clean: On the table was spread a white cloth, and there were seven little bowls filled with sardines—"good omega-3s, man," she noted—and seven little glasses that curiously held salt water, and seven knives and forks laid in order. Along the wall stood seven little beds, each with its own igloo canopy of ice blocks. As she was very hungry, she ate one single fish from each bowl, and after that she thought she would take a rest. A finicky sleeper, she tried all the little beds, finding that one was too long, and another was too short, till at last the seventh suited her perfectly. It was a waterbed. "Groovy," she purred as she laid herself down and let the little waves rock her to sleep.

By and by, the owners of the cottage returned. They were seven little prospecting penguins that worked in the nearby mountains, digging for gold. The unsuspecting Antarctic birds entered their dark abode, lighted up their seven lamps as usual, but saw right away that all was not right. [Editor's Note: We've translated the following from penguin.]

The first said, "Who has been eating my sardines?"

The second said, "Who has been eating *my* sardines?"

The third said, "Who has been eating *my* sardines?"

The fourth said, "Who has been eating *my* sardines?"

The fifth said, "Who has been eating *my* sardines?"

The sixth said, "Who has been eating *my* sardines?"

The seventh said, "It's actually not a prob for me. I'm sorta burned out on fish."

Then the first waddled over to his igloo and said, "Who has been lying on my bed?"

"And mine—"

"And mine—"

"And mine—"

"And mine—"

"And mine—"

"And—yoo-hoo, guys?"

The rest bobbled over with their lamps to the seventh, who had found that somebody had not only been upon his bed, but somebody was actually *still in it*. "That's too big for a bedbug, right?"

It was no bedbug: It was our girl Snowdrop, sleeping soundly.

The penguins crowded around the bed and honked with wonder and astonishment as they looked at her. "Good heavens!" said one. "What a lovely child she is!"

said another. And rather than waking her, the seventh penguin slept an hour on each of the other penguins' beds in turn, till the night was over.

In the morning, over krill omelets, Snowdrop told them the whole story. " . . . And that was, like, how I ended up here." The penguins were moved by her plight and made a deal that if she would play guitar and sing for them often, she could stay right where she was, and they promised to take good care of her.

Then they went out all day long to their work, seeking gold and silver in the mountains. Before they left, they warned her, "Be careful. That stepmother of yours will come after you the moment she hears you're still alive. So don't open the door to anyone!"

Snowdrop nodded, and though they thought it was in somber agreement with their warning, it was more about locking in the right tempo for the new tune she was composing in her head.

Meanwhile, back at the castle, the queen, thinking Snowdrop was a goner, approached her glass with a confident swagger and said:

"Tell me, old coots, tell me true!
Of all the ladies in the land,
Who is fairest? Spill it: WHO?"

And the two guys in the glass answered:

"Well, queen, you're the fairest in all this land:
But over the hills, in the forest shade,
Where the seven penguins ply their trade,
There Snowdrop is hiding her head;
And she is far lovelier, oh queen, than you."

Piggy was instantly livid. "That doesn't even *rhyme!*"
But she couldn't come up with a second or third
point, because she knew that Statler and Waldorf were
compelled by the spell to speak the truth, and she was
sure that Stephen had betrayed her. She could not bear to
think that anyone who lived was more beautiful than she
was. Finally, she concluded, "If you want a dastardly job
done right, you do it your dastardly self, right?"

Down she dashed to the castle's dungeon lab, to call
on the court doctor, Bunsen Honeydew, and his assistant,
Beaker. "I need something deadly, a substance that no
one would suspect was harmful," she demanded. "And
whatever you devise must be delivered by something so
attractive, a pretty girl couldn't refuse it."

"Oh, I'm far too busy to go myself," Honeydew
demurred, joking. Beaker tittered, but the queen just
stared at the doc, so he got serious again and continued.

"We've been experimenting with something that I think will make you very happy." He held up a shiny, pen-shaped metal container coated in a mouth-watering apple-red varnish.

"Do tell," said Piggy, intrigued . . .

That afternoon, the queen disguised herself as an old peddler, went over the hills to the place where the penguins dwelt, and knocked at the door.

Snowdrop peeked out a window and said, "Like, hi, Old Peddler. What are you selling?"

"The finest cosmetics," said the costumed queen, whom Snowdrop did not recognize.

"But I'm not allowed to open the door to anyone."

"I'm harmless. I'm just a makeup specialist."

"How did you get all the way out here?"

"Why, in my *compact* car, naturally!"

"Like, sorry, but I don't get puns."

Persistent Piggy changed her tack. "Woo wee, it is so hot out here. I feel faint!"

Uh-oh, I oughta let the poor old lady in, she needs help, thought the compassionate singer to herself as she ran to unbolt the door.

"Bless me! I feel better already," said the visitor, stepping over the threshold. *Drat*, thought Piggy as she scrutinized Snowdrop's face. *She is pretty*. "But my goodness, look how badly your eyeliner is applied! Let me introduce you to a liner called Drop Dead, Gorgeous."

"Okay, fer sure." Snowdrop did not dream of any mischief, so she stood still as the old woman set to work drawing the tainted liner around her eyes. Almost in an instant, Snowdrop's breath stopped, and down she fell as if she were dead.

"Beauty may only be skin deep," purred the spiteful queen, "but this poison sure penetrates!" And she turned tail and hustled home.

In the evening the seven penguins returned, and I need not say how grieved they were to see their beloved Snowdrop stretched out upon the ground, as if she was quite finished, though with very artfully defined eyes. However, they lifted her into a chair and, suspecting this unfamiliar makeup might be the trouble, they wiped off the evil eyeliner. Soon Snowdrop began to breathe and eventually came to life again, and she told them what had transpired.

Said one penguin, "The old woman was the queen in disguise—I'm sure of it!" Added another from behind him, "Take care and don't let anyone in when we're away." Said a third from the supper table, "Oh, come on, guys: fish for dinner *again*?"

When Piggy got home, she went straight to her glass,

confident the problem had been remedied, and spoke to it as before. But to her great surprise and grief, Statler and Waldorf said:

> *"Well, queen, you're the fairest in all this land:*
> *But far away and deep in the trees,*
> *Where the seven penguins do as they please,*
> *There Snowdrop is hiding her head;*
> *And she is far lovelier, oh queen, than you."*

"You two have *got* to work harder on your rhymes!" Piggy hissed through clenched teeth. Her blood ran cold with spite and malice to know that the low blow to her foe resulted in no woe. "Oh, what a pain in the assonance!" She marched down to the dungeon and told Honeydew and Beaker that their first ploy flopped and Snowdrop somehow had survived.

Honeydew pivoted to peer at his assistant. "Beaker, you look so unkempt today. Did you even comb your hair?" The confused carrottop brought a hand to his crabgrass coif and meekly offered a *"meep"* of apology. Honeydew handed him a comb, and the very moment Beaker touched it to his unruly orange mop, he fell down as if dead.

A slow grin spread across Piggy's face.

She dressed herself up again, but in quite another costume from the one she wore before, and took with her the poisoned comb. She knocked at the door of the penguins' cottage and cried, "Combs for sale!"

Inside, wary Snowdrop leaned against the door and wisely replied, "The penguins said not to let anyone in."

"You don't have to let me in," assured the queen. "But please just take a look at my beautiful comb!" And she slid it under the door.

"Wow, you're not kidding," said Snowdrop, picking up the tortoiseshell marvel. The poison was so powerful that the moment the comb touched her long blond hair, she dropped to the floor.

From the other side of the door Piggy heard the thud. "I can't believe she really *fell* for that," said the delighted queen, and went on her way.

Because of a brewing storm, the penguins happened to quit work early that evening and returned home. When they saw Snowdrop lying on the ground next to a comb none of them recognized, they could guess what had happened. After they donned hazmat suits and took the comb away and burned it, Snowdrop got well, and told them all that had passed. They warned her once again not to open the door to anyone.

In the meantime, the queen stood before her glass and

shook with rage when she heard the very same answer as before. She returned to the court chemists. "I need some outside-the-box thinking, buster," she said to Honeydew.

"How about inside-the-basket?" he replied, holding out a woven-twig bushel of kumquats to her.

She shook her head. "Oh, no thank you, I'm dieting. In fact, I took up exercising by riding horses."

"Is it working?"

"Is it ever: In three weeks the horse has lost thirty pounds!"

"Well," Honeydew continued, "these kumquats are bona fide killers. As you can see, the outside looks very orange and tempting, but they pack a lethal punch."

"She'll be suspicious by now," said Piggy. "What if she wants me to taste one first, to prove it's not poison?"

"Oh yes, I've thought of that already. There is a trick: The kumquat is devised so that one side, with a slightly darker orange color, is perfectly normal, while the other side, with a lighter orange color, will terminate you in a blink. Go on, Beaker, show Queen Piggy how it works." Honeydew handed his assistant one of the kumquats.

Beaker looked at it, wary. *"Meep meep, meep meep?"*

"Yes, that side is the correct one." Beaker peered skeptically at the fruit as Honeydew insisted. "*Yes*, I'm quite certain that side is safe. I stake my entire reputation on it."

Beaker took a bite of the kumquat and—bam!—hit the floor, senseless.

"Oh, silly me, I must have gotten that mixed up. Luckily I never had much of a reputation to begin with!"

Piggy dressed herself up as a peasant's wife—boy, was her costume closet *stocked*—and traveled over the hills to the penguins' cottage, where she knocked at the door. But Snowdrop poked her head out the window and said quite resolutely, "Sorry, poor person, but I rilllly can't let anyone in, 'cause the tuxedo birds told me not to."

"Do as you please," said the old woman, approaching the window, "but do take this pretty kumquat."

"Ooo, kumquats are the yummiest. I can't resist 'em," said Snowdrop. "But like, I totally have to say no thanks."

"You silly girl!" answered the incognito queen, laughing lightly, "what are you afraid of? Do you think it's poisoned or something? I'll show you that's not true." She took a bite out of it, and Janice, seeing that it did the old crone no harm, could wait no longer and took one from the basket. As soon as she popped it into her mouth, she fell down upon the ground as if dead. "This time nothing will save you," said the queen, with an evil cackle she cribbed from Vincent Price in the "Thriller" video. She went home to her glass, and at last Statler and Waldorf said:

"Happy news! It's our enchanted duty
To report you're once again the #1 beauty."

And then her wicked heart was as glad as such a heart could be.

When evening came and the penguins had gone home, they found Snowdrop lying on the ground. No breath came from her lips! "Either this girl is not very smart or she just has terrible luck," said one exasperated bird.

Another shook his head. "Personally, I don't think it's an 'either/or' kind of situation."

They administered all the CPR they could remember: they palpated her heart, splashed water on her face, flapped her arms like emu wings—but all was in vain, for the young woman seemed quite dead.

So, according to Antarctic-penguin tradition, they laid her in a coffin made of ice and set it upon the ground in a cool glade near their house. The penguin who happened to be the worst speller wrote upon it in golden letters SNOWDORP. And thus she lay for a long, long time, looking as though she was only asleep, for she was even now as pale as snow, and as red as blood, and as yellow as birch wood.

At last a prince happened by on his horse. Red of beard and hippie of attire, Floyd Pepper saw Snowdrop lying there and pulled the reins. He dismounted. He raised his sunglasses. Instantly smitten, he took his guitar from his saddlebag and improvised a song for this strange, beautiful, sleeping lady. He played so passionately that the penguins came from the cottage to watch. He rocked out so hard that the vibrations of the music made the ground shake. The shaking dislodged the undetected piece of kumquat in Snowdrop's mouth, and out it fell from between her lips. She awoke and sat up, bonking her head on the ice coffin lid. "Where am I?" she wondered. "And also, ouch."

Floyd broke through the ice with the neck of his guitar and said, "Hey there, pretty little lady. You're safe and sound. I love you far better than all the world, so come with me to my father's palace. You can be my wife and we'll make some groovy music together. So, what's the sitch: Will you marry me?"

And Snowdrop, knowing the import of such a question and the monumental decision she faced, considered carefully and delivered her thoughtful reply: "Yeah, sure!"

The penguins all cheered and threw one another into the air in celebration.

Snowdrop traveled home with the prince and everything was prepared with great pomp and splendor for their wedding. Her stepmother, Queen Piggy, was asked to attend, and since Snowdrop was listed on the invitation by her birth name "Janice," Piggy had no idea who the bride was. As always, she RSVP'd yes right away, writing on the reply card, "I *never* miss an occasion for a chocolate fondue fountain!"

As she was dressing for the event in a Prada outfit that had been FedExed after the dirndl outrage, she looked in the glass and posed her standard question, eager for her usual confidence boost:

"Tell me, old coots, tell me true!
Of all the ladies in the land,
Who is fairest? Spill it: WHO?"

And the gents in the glass answered:

"The loveliest right here? In this room? You are.
But elsewhere, the soon-to-be queen Janice is lovelier by far."

When her monumental temper tantrum ended, her envy and curiosity were still so great that she could not help attending the nuptials anyway, just to peep the bride. When Piggy arrived and reached out to dip a strawberry in the cascading chocolate sauce, she saw that it was no other than Snowdrop—*SNOWDROP!*— who she thought had been dead a long while, and her heart burst with rage and she fell down and died. ("Yeah right," she said, warily lifting her head and cracking an eyelid, "until you need someone to play the *next* villain, amirite?")

For many, many years to come, Snowdrop and Floyd lived and reigned over that land. Often, they went up into the mountains and paid a visit to the little penguins, who had always been so kind to Snowdrop even after she did the absolute dimmest things.

And there in that cottage, on the couch, Snowdrop would always think of her long-gone queen mother when she looked at the throw pillow she inherited: the embroidered kitten hanging from a tree branch beneath the phrase HANG IN THERE. Which her little Janice somehow always managed to do.

Faithful Sweetums

AFTER "FAITHFUL JOHN"

One day long ago in Italy, old queen Mama Fiama was languishing near death on her sickbed. Her periwinkle complexion had paled to powder blue, and her silver hair, loosed from its usual bun, almost matched the shiny satin pillowcase. She had woken in the middle of the night and said to an attendant, "Tell-a faithful Sweetums to come to me."

Faithful Sweetums was a great woolly ogre with an imposing face but a sensitive spirit. The gentle giant had been loyal to the queen and her only son his whole life, and won Employee of the Month more often than any of the other palace workers. When he lumbered to her bedside that night, wearing the tattered brown shirt he loved so, cowlicks sticking up willy-nilly all over his hairy head and face, the queen said to him in her lilting Italian accent, "My most-a faithful Sweetums, I hope-a you weren't a-sleeping."

"Noooo," he said in his gravelly voice, only half fibbing. "Ogres always sleep with one eye open. It freaks people out, but keeps us prepared at all times."

She took one of his mammoth paws into her tiny hands. "Why I call-a you tonight is this: I feel-a that my end may be near. My only concern is-a for my boy, The Great Gonzo. I love-a him so, but he is still young and doesn't always have the most good . . . how you say . . . *judgment.* Just last week I find-a him using tennis rackets to water-ski around the moat." She shook her head. "That don't-a work." She peered intently at Sweetums. "I will not be able to close-a my eyes in peace if you do not promise to be like his foster father and teach-a him everything that he ought to know."

"Yar," faithful Sweetums answered, his big lower lip set in resolve. "I will not forsake him, and will serve him always, no matter what."

"Even if it cost-a you your life?"

"Even then."

At this, old queen Mama Fiama was greatly relieved. "Then I just have-a two more things I ask-a you to do before I go ciao-ciao. First: After my death, show-a to Gonzo the entire castle—all-a the chambers, halls, and vaults, and all-a the treasures they have in them. But," she paused and waggled a bony finger in warning, "do *not* show-a him the last chamber in the main hallway upstairs."

"Why not?"

"Inside is-a the portrait of Princess Camilla the Chicken. You and me, we both know-a how much Gonzo like-a the fair fowls, and we also know-a how if he get too excited he go—how you say?"

"Unconscious."

"*Sì!* If my Gonzo see-a that picture? Oh, I just-a know he will-a fall forever in love with Camilla. And she is-a notoriously choosy. She has tell 'no' to every suitor that ever try-a to win her. Sweetums, protect-a my boy from-a heartbreak, *capisci*?"

"I understand," he said, nodding his huge head. It created a breeze that gently ruffled the old lady's hair. "And the last thing you need of me?"

"Polenta!"

"Polenta?"

"The cornmeal that I boil and shape-a into patties, then fry and serve with a nice creamy mushroom sauce. You make-a the polenta for Gonzo, yes? He is so picky but he love-a the corn. Is his favorite. I have-a hoarded three tons of kernels that Mr. Miller the village miller will-a grind for you. You will never run out. And you use-a that to make-a the polenta. I already e-mail you the recipe."

Faithful Sweetums gave his promise to the old queen about this, and she said no more. She laid her head on her pillow and took her last breath, leaving Gonzo to became king of the land. Like his mom, Gonzo had a royal blue hue, though he must have inherited his father's very prominent schnoz. It was *big*—he could eat a banana in the rain without it ever getting wet.

After a sufficient period of mourning had passed, faithful Sweetums told Gonzo almost all that he had promised his mother on her deathbed. He placed a hand on his charge's shoulder and said, "I will keep my word to Mama Fiama, and I will make you polenta, and I will be loyal to you as I have been loyal to her, even if it should cost me my life."

"Cool!" said Gonzo.

"It is now time for you to receive your inheritance. Are you ready to see everything in your mother's castle?" Sweetums then took him everywhere—everywhere *except* that one chamber that contained the dangerous portrait of the oh-so-tempting chicken.

Later, as they walked along the upstairs hallway, Gonzo stopped in front of the door of the unseen chamber, with a curious look on his face. "Hey, Sweetums," he said, "how come you didn't open this one for me?"

"Uhhhhh," Sweetums stalled, trying to think up

an excuse. "There is something in there . . . that would frighten you."

That was clearly the wrong answer. "Ooo, I love scary stuff," said the new king, his interest supremely piqued.

Faithful Sweetums stepped between Gonzo and the door, blocking it with his bulk. "I promised Mama Fiama before her death that you wouldn't see inside this chamber. She warned me that it could put us both in very big trouble."

"I can't help feeling," continued Gonzo, not really listening, "that if I don't go in, it's gonna drive me mental. I won't be able to sleep until I've seen inside with my own two peepers. So either you unlock that door, or I break it down! And you're looking at the guy who once slingshotted himself into a three-story tower of Twinkies just for fun."

Sweetums said nothing, so Gonzo backed up and took a run at the door. He smashed against it with his shoulder, letting out a little yelp—the solid door didn't even rattle. "That wood is waaaay more dense than sponge cake," said Gonzo, smarting. "I might have to rethink my strategy."

Sweetums knew the king would not rest until he'd been admitted into the room, so the ogre located the key on the large ring he wore around his wide waist and inserted it into the lock. The door creaked open, releasing an unnaturally cool draft of air. Sweetums marveled at the portrait of Princess Camilla that hung on the far wall. It was so masterfully executed that the bewitching bird seemed to live and breathe and to be the most charming, beautiful thing in the whole world. But his plan to obscure the view from Gonzo was foiled, because before he knew it, the curious king had climbed up onto the ogre's broad shoulders and laid eyes on the portrait.

Gonzo was gobsmacked: The painting was so magnificent—rendered in rich oils and studded with gold and precious stones—that, just as old Mama Fiama had predicted, he fell with a thud to the ground, unconscious.

For the next few days Sweetums nursed the pale king with matzo ball soup and Pedialyte until he regained full consciousness and his wan complexion had returned to its usual robust blue. Once he had his strength back, Gonzo's first utterance was "Wowza." His next words were "Hubba hubba!" He sat up in bed and rubbed his eyes. "Whose portrait is that that knocked me out cold?"

"That is Princess Camilla the Chicken," answered faithful Sweetums, chagrined.

"I've always had a thing for feathered females," Gonzo continued. "But this Camilla! My love for her is so great that if all the leaves on all the trees were tongues, they would still not be able to express it! I mean, look at that: She's got me spouting poetry! The last time I spouted anything was when I put that fire hose in my ear and tried to turn myself into a lawn sprinkler." He grabbed Sweetums by the shoulders. "I will risk my life to win her, I tell ya. You are my most faithful friend. You just gotta help me."

The servant nodded and told Gonzo he'd come up with a plan by dinnertime. And as promised, over their usual supper of polenta with a creamy mushroom sauce, Sweetums spelled out the scheme. "All chickens love corn, just as you do," he explained. "And Mama Fiama left you three tons of it. Strange as it may sound, I suggest you have the local artisans fashion that corn into all manner of statues and sculptures, then decorate them with corn kernels, tortilla chips, popcorn, and so on. Since chickens love corn, any chicken would find that irresistible, and maybe Camilla will find you irresistible, too."

"That's the weirdest idea ever," marveled Gonzo. "I love it! Count me in."

They quickly summoned the kingdom's artisans, a clever and creative group of tireless arachnids who called themselves the Village Spiders. They worked around the clock until, at last, they had finished the most splendid, corn-covered enticements. When everything had been loaded aboard a ship, Gonzo and Sweetums had the crew sail them across the sea toward France until they came to the port city of Cock-a-doodle-Deauville, where Princess Camilla ruled from her opulent henhouse on a cliff overlooking the ocean.

Faithful Sweetums insisted Gonzo stay behind on the ship and wait for him (no sense risking the king falling down unconscious again) and carried with him a corn-encrusted bust of George Clooney as he went ashore and walked straight to the royal coop.

The princess Camilla was lunching on an earthworm, and when she saw Sweetums she was startled. But noticing the corny likeness of the Oscar-winning humanitarian in his hands, she couldn't help but be intrigued. She called out in greeting, *"Bgark cluck cluck bawwwwk!"*

Faithful Sweetums didn't speak chicken, so he said, "I am just the servant of a rich king. This piece I have here is not to be compared with those my master has in his ship. They are the most beautiful and delicious things you could imagine." Curious Camilla consented to go with him to see it all for herself. Once they arrived at the ship, Gonzo appeared and said, "Hello, beautiful princess. I'm prepared to hear your every wish." He pointed to his green suit, which was sewn entirely from freshly shorn corn husks. "Seriously—I'm all ears!" She clucked bashfully and fluttered her lashes at him.

Gonzo whispered to the ogre, "She's even more beautiful than the portrait! I think my heart might break—and that might be the only part of my body I *haven't* broken at some point."

At Gonzo's eager invitation, the hen scampered up the gangplank to the ship, and he bashfully led her inside the hull. Faithful Sweetums remained with the helmsman, Mad Monty, and as part of the preordained plan, he ordered the ship to set sail once again for home.

Belowdecks, Camilla remained oblivious as Gonzo wowed her with all the uncanny corn creations. "Feel free to sample anything you want," he suggested, and she did as he wished, pecking at some of the kernels and savoring the robust flavor. After she had her fill, she thanked her eagerly attentive if uniquely featured host and returned to the deck so that she could disembark. But she let out an alarmed *"BGARK!"* when she saw that the ship was already far out to sea, and speeding onward at full sail!

Taking her by the wing and leading her to a cozy haystack he had prepared for this circumstance, Gonzo said, "I suppose I'd better come clean, my dear Camilla. I might have tricked you into coming with me, but it's only because of my great love for you. I mean, the first time I saw your portrait, I fell to the ground unconscious.

I've never seen a more beautiful creature. And I figured there was no way you'd find a strange-looking whatever like me attractive."

Though Gonzo wasn't the first to try to win her with compliments, she roosted on the hay anyway, flattered. He *was* a strange-looking whatever, but she did, in fact, find him attractive.

"I'm willing to do whatever it takes to woo you, Camilla. There's nothing I'd like more in the world than to spend my life happily henpecked." He dropped to one knee and took out a ring box. Surprised, she put a wing to her beak and inhaled sharply. Inside the box was a metal band. Gonzo asked, "Princess Camilla, will you marry me?" And with a gentle touch, he placed the band around her leg. In that instant, the chicken's heart yielded, and she consented to be his wife.

Now it so happened that while they were sailing along the high sea, faithful Sweetums, who was sitting at the front of the ship strumming his lute—

"Lyre!" yelled Mad Monty from belowdecks.

Oops, he's right—it wasn't a lute, it was indeed a lyre.

So there Sweetums was, strumming his lyre, when he saw three seabirds flying toward them. He was an avid birder, so by their markings he recognized them as an Ohboy, a Forcryingoutloud, and a Whattayasay. The trio landed on one of the masts. Sweetums stopped playing and eavesdropped on their conversation, for though he didn't speak chicken, he was fluent in seabird.

One of them said, "Oh boy! Gonzo has won Princess Camilla."

"For crying out loud," replied the second, "it's not a done deal yet."

"Whatta ya say?" asked the third. "She's roosting beside him right there on the ship, with a wedding band around her leg."

Then the first bird spoke again: "Oh boy, what good will any of that do him? When they reach land, Melville the whale will surface to meet him, and the adventure-loving king will want the big fish to ferry them to shore. But if they climb aboard, it will descend into the murky depths and Gonzo and his bride will perish!"

The second one exclaimed, "For crying out loud! Is there no way he can avoid that?"

"Oh boy, is there ever—if someone else quickly drops the anchor onto the whale's head, then the young king and his love will be rescued. But who knows that? Nobody! And if anyone *does* know it, and if they tell it to the king, he will be turned to stone from his toes to his knees," the first bird said.

Then the second bird said, "For crying out loud! I

know more than that. Even if someone smacks the whale, still the young king will not keep his bride."

"Whatta ya say?"

"When they enter the castle together," the first bird continued, "a handmade wedding shirt will be lying there on a tray. It will look like it's woven of gold and silver, but it is nothing but sulfur and pitch. If he puts it on, it will burn him to the very marrow of his bones." [Editor's Note: There's a "haute couture" joke somewhere in here but we're not gonna be the ones to try it.]

"For crying out loud, there is *one* way out of this," replied the second seabird. "If someone wearing gloves grabs the garment, and throws it into the fire and burns it up, then the young king will be saved. And what good will that do? If anyone knows this and tells it to the king, half his body will become stone, from his knees to his heart."

Then the third bird said, "I know more than you. Even if the wedding shirt is burned up, the young king will *still* not have his bride. After the wedding, when the queen is dancing, she will suddenly turn pale and fall flat on her face. If someone doesn't lift her up and blow three breaths into her beak right away, she will die. But if anyone who knows that reveals it, his entire body will turn to stone, from the crown of his head to the soles of his feet."

"Oh boy, these old German folktale plots sure get convoluted," said the first seabird. "Anyone up for the buffet at the sandbar? It's all-you-can-eat escargot!"

The other two enthusiastically agreed.

"I hope my old boyfriend isn't there," said the second. "He never leaves me alone! I guess I should have known better than to date an albatross."

"Well, I, for one, am ready to mingle," said the first.

The third clicked its tongue. "You go, gull!" And off they flew.

Faithful Sweetums had heard and understood all their terrible prophecies. He became quiet and sad, for if he concealed what he had heard from Gonzo, it would bring misfortune to the king, but if he revealed it to him, then he himself would be turned to stone. Finally, with Mama Fiama in his mind, he made his decision: "I will save my master, even if it brings destruction on myself."

When the ship arrived back in Italy, what the seabirds foretold did indeed happen, and a magnificent whale surfaced. "Melville!" cried Gonzo in greeting. "He can carry us to the castle. Hop on, Camilla! Just mind the barnacles."

He was about to climb onto the whale's back when faithful Sweetums dropped the ship's anchor and smacked the massive mammal squarely on the head. The king's other servants, who had always been snooty to Sweetums because of Mama Fiama's favoritism, stood onshore and grumbled. Said one, "How whacko to attack the beautiful animal that was to have ferried the king to shore."

But Gonzo said to them, "Hold your tongues. Leave him alone. He is my most faithful Sweetums. Who knows what good may come of this?"

They entered the castle, and in the hall there sat a tray on which lay the wedding shirt, which appeared to be made of gold and silver. Young King Gonzo was about to pick it up, but faithful Sweetums suddenly seized it with gloves, carried it quickly to the fire, and burned it.

The other servants were again scandalized. Griped one, "What a crackpot, burning up the king's wedding shirt."

But the young king said, "He probably had a reason. Leave him alone. He is my most faithful Sweetums."

Soon the wedding took place. After the vows, Marvin Suggs played his Muppaphone, and everyone began dancing. Camilla loved to cut a rug. Faithful Sweetums was nervous and watchful, and, just as predicted, the chicken suddenly turned pale and fell on her face as if she were dead. He ran quickly to her, picked her up, and carried her into a chamber. He laid her down and blew air into her beak three times. Immediately she regained consciousness.

Gonzo watched from the doorway, his jealousy inflamed, not knowing why Sweetums would do such a thing. In his rage, he shouted, "That's enough! Throw him into prison!" And the other servants were more than happy to do the king's bidding.

The next morning Sweetums was led to the gallows by Gonzo and the court. Standing high on the platform and on the verge of being executed, the ogre said, "Everyone who is condemned to die is permitted before his end to say one last thing. May I also have this right?"

"Of course," answered Gonzo. "I'm feeling kinda lousy about my outburst yesterday. Maybe I overreacted just a tad with all of this."

Faithful Sweetums said, "I have been unjustly condemned, and have always been loyal to you," and he related how he had heard the conversation of the seabirds, and how he had needed to do all these bizarre things in an effort to save his master.

Gonzo was instantly flooded with remorse. "Ohhhhh, how sorry I am, my most faithful Sweetums. I'm pardoning you! And, Sweetums, I hope you'll please now pardon me!" But his request fell on deaf ears, for faithful Sweetums was already lifeless and turned into stone.

This caused the king and his chicken queen great

grief. Gonzo ordered the stone figure to be hoisted up and placed in his bedroom next to his bed. Nearby, Camilla roosted on a pallet of hay, keeping a pair of soon-to-hatch eggs warm. Every time that Gonzo looked at his marbleized old friend he wept, saying, "Oh, if only I could bring you back to life again, my most faithful pal."

One day, when Camilla was out of the room, the stone replied, saying to Gonzo, "You can bring me back to life again if you will in return give up what is dearest to you." It sounded just like Sweetums's voice! Gonzo, amazed, exclaimed, "For you I will give up everything I have in the world!"

"To break the spell, you must crack Camilla's eggs on me."

"Wait—what?!"

"I know it sounds insane, but if you do this, I will be restored to life."

The king was perplexed. Camilla would be furious. But he thought of faithful Sweetums's great loyalty, and how he had turned to stone for him, and he felt he had no choice. So he picked up the eggs from the nest and threw them against the statue, thereby killing two birds with one stone, as it were. Suddenly the statue transformed, and faithful Sweetums stood before him, again healthy and well.

The reanimated ogre said to the king, "Your loyalty shall not go unrewarded," and then he fitted the eggshells together like a puzzle, and suddenly they were whole again. Minutes later both hatched and out jumped two adorable yellow chicks. They giggled at Sweetums, wiping runny egg from his eye. Said one, "The yoke's on you!"

From then on, the entire household lived in harmony. Gonzo and Camilla and their chicks were content. Sweetums retired and was henceforth treated as part of the family. He didn't even have to make the meals anymore—they'd hired a full-time cook, a Swedish chef, who, despite his Nordic heritage and the formidable language barrier, made an absolutely top-notch polenta with mushroom sauce that'd even please Mama Fiama.

Unclestiltskin

AFTER "RUMPELSTILTSKIN"

Once there was a guy named Mr. Miller who, as it happened, was a miller. Mr. Miller's mill may not have made him much money, but it sure produced plenty of alliteration. He lived there with an intelligent and confident daughter he called Piggy, who, as it happened, was a pig.

Now it also happened that one day he had to go and speak to the king, who was known around the land by the name of Dr. Teeth. On their agenda was an order of flour for an upcoming all-kingdom feast, and the miller's insistent daughter asked to tag along. "You know how obsessed I am with crowns and courts and palaces. And the closest I've ever gotten to that is White Castle."

"Fine," her father said, "but whatever you do, *at all costs*, do NOT say anything embarrassing." When they appeared before His Majesty, her father suddenly short-circuited at the sight of all that opulence and blurted out, "My daughter Piggy here can spin straw into gold!"

With an epic eye roll, Piggy muttered, "I'm sure glad I didn't say anything embarrassing."

But instead of laughing off the now-mortified miller's wild claim, His Majesty Dr. Teeth exclaimed "Outtasight!" He broke into a brilliant smile, showing off a set of piano key–size choppers, all immaculately white save one, which was encased in the finest of gold. "As you cats can see from my totally groovy dental work, I'm partial to precious metal. And after all, what's a king without a crown?" From somewhere in the castle, a drummer played a rimshot. "Band rehearsal in the rec room," Teeth explained. "Anyway, my dentist says I'll be needing a lot more of these gold caps if I wanna avoid dentures. So, my main man, if your daughter is as uniquely skilled as you say, let's put the little lady to the test."

Dr. Teeth sent Mr. Miller home and took Piggy to a room high in the castle that was quite full of straw and little else, save a spinning wheel. He said, "If by tomorrow morning at sunrise you haven't spun all this straw into gold during the night, well, I'm sorry, it's tradition, but you're gonna hafta die. So, power to the people, and night night!" Thereupon he abruptly exited, closing the door behind him and leaving her alone in the room.

"Did he say *die*?" Piggy wondered aloud to herself.

"Maybe he meant 'dye,' as in change my hair color."

"Nope," said a small voice. Piggy turned to the corner it came from and peered closer: It was an insect. "Name's Jacques Roach," it continued. "I've lived in the castle crevices for a long time and you're not the first spinner Dr. Teeth has tested."

"What happened to the others?"

"Uhhh, would it make you feel better if I said they changed their hair color?"

Panicked, Piggy tried the door handle—locked! She looked for a window—none! She tried her cell phone— no signal! She plopped down on a stool. "I have no idea how to spin straw into gold!"

"I wish I could help, but I'm too tiny to operate the spinning wheel. But if this goes like it has in the past, I think you should be expecting a visitor right about—"

All at once the door opened, and in trundled a blue creature with a pair of curved horns atop his alligator-like head, wearing a tattered brown suit from a bygone era. He spoke in a proper English accent, his tongue working around a set of dagger-sharp teeth: "Good evening, Mistress Miller."

"Hello, strange reptilian lizard thing," answered the pig.

He moved closer. "Why are you crying so?"

"That king with the flashy grill and red chinstrap beard has ordered *moi* to spin this straw into gold. The only spinning I've done involves a stationary bike, and I don't do that very well." She sighed. "The other day in class I peddled backward and put on ten pounds!"

The creature peered at her with his beady, pea-green eyes. "What will you give me if I do it for you?"

"How about my phone?" She held it out to him.

"A BlackBerry?! You can't be serious, dear."

Unseen, Jacques had scrambled up onto her shoulder and now whispered in her ear, "Offer him a riddle!"

She figured she had nothing to lose. "What if I told you a riddle?"

"Well, I do value a witty brainteaser. Try me."

Piggy listened intently as Jacques whispered in her ear, then repeated: "If a silkworm makes silk, and a moth makes holes, then what would you have if you crossed the two of them?"

The visitor was intrigued. "I give up."

"You'd have a bug that makes lace!"

"Ooo, very clever. Brava." Satisfied, he seated himself in front of the wheel, and *whirr, whirr, whirr*, three turns, and just like that, the reel was full of golden threads. Then he put another on, and *whirr, whirr, whirr*, the second reel was full, too.

And so Piggy's curious helper spun into the night, and the whirring of the wheel sent her to sleep faster than her white-noise app. When she woke at daybreak, the creature and all the straw were gone and the reels were full of gold. Dr. Teeth was standing there, gobsmacked at the 24-karat vision before him. "Sock it to me!" He was delighted, and his heart became only more greedy. He had the miller's daughter taken into a larger room full of straw and commanded her to again spin it all in one night if she valued her life.

Locked in, the pig knew not how to help herself and was fuming when the door opened and in walked alligator head. He said, "What will you give me if I spin that straw into gold for you?"

When this time he agreed to her offer of a joke, Jacques again crept up onto Piggy's shoulder and she parroted back what he whispered to her: "Two boll weevils came from the country to the city. One became rich and famous. The other remained the lesser of two weevils!"

The blue creature laughed, quite pleased, and again began to turn the wheel. By morning he had spun all the straw into glittering gold and disappeared again. Dr. Teeth rejoiced beyond measure at the sight but still wanted more. He took the miller's daughter to the largest room yet, stacked to the rafters with straw. "I think I see where this is headed," sighed a weary Piggy.

She was right. But he added something surprising to the usual drill: "This time if you succeed," he announced, "we'll get hitched."

"Wait—seriously?" said Piggy. "That means I'd be queen, right?"

"Right on."

The dangled carrot suddenly seemed like the most delicious thing on earth. When she was alone, the blue creature came again, and for the third time said, "What will you give me if—"

Piggy knew the routine by now and interrupted. "A joke! I'll give you another joke! Then I get to become queen and finally get the wardrobe I deserve!"

"I want *more* than a joke though," he said, a new note of mischief in his voice. "This time, you must promise me that if you should become queen, you'll give me . . . the royal dog!"

Piggy was puzzled. "The royal dog?" She thought to herself, *Who knows whether we'll get a pet or not?* And so she promised the prehistoric-looking pest what he wanted. With that, he once more spun the straw into gold.

Next morning, Dr. Teeth walked in and found all as he had wished. "With all this gold I can finally mellow out." He dropped to his knee and said, "Fine lady, will you—"

"I will, I will, I will!" she blurted, and with that, the pretty pig achieved her ultimate wish, to become a queen.

A year later, the royal duo adopted a scruffy white

dog from the pound. They named her Foo-Foo. And Piggy never gave a thought to that strange savior who'd appeared so serendipitously in the spinning room—until suddenly one day she found him lurking in her quarters.

"Now you must give me what you promised," he declared.

Piggy was horror-struck, for she had fallen quite in love with Foo-Foo. She offered the gold-spinning demon all the riches of the kingdom if he would let her keep the pooch. But the creature refused. Then the queen began to lament and cry so much that he pitied her. "All right, all right. I will offer you the chance to change our agreement," said he. "I will give you three days, and if by that time you manage to find out my name, then you shall keep your dog."

"That's all? Just find out your name?"

"My name. And if you fail, the hound goes home with me."

So Piggy spent the whole night Googling, jotting down all the names she ran across, and just to be safe, she asked Jacques Roach to inquire far and wide for any particularly obscure options.

When the blue menace showed up the next day, the queen began her guessing with "Frank," "José," "Manish," and other familiar names from around the world, then on to less-used monikers like "Caspar,"

"Melchior," and "Balthazar," one after another. But to every try the creature shook his head and replied, with a smug expression, "That is not my name."

On the second day, Piggy crowdsourced the question on Facebook and Twitter, and just to be safe, she also had Jacques scurry around the neighboring kingdoms for the names of the people there. When the creature appeared that evening, she repeated the most uncommon and curious of them. "Perhaps your name is Shortribs, or Sheepshanks, or Wiggleleg?"

But he always answered, "That is not my name."

On the third day, Jacques came back from surveying the kingdoms outside the neighboring kingdoms. He was exhausted from his travels, with all six feet covered in blisters. "I haven't been able to find a single new name," he reported. "But as I came to a high mountain at the end of the forest—after passing six baby bandits, seven gold-digging penguins, and a partridge in a pear tree—I saw a little house shrouded in mist, and in front of the house a fire was burning. And lo and behold, around that fire I saw the ridiculous blue dinosaur thingy jumping and hopping upon one leg." He relayed its curious chant:

"Tonight I dance in the thick fog,
But tomorrow I'll finally win that dog.

Oh, how hard it is to play my game,
For Unclestiltskin is my name!"

You may imagine how glad Queen Piggy was to learn this. And when soon afterward the creature showed up with his brand-new leash and doggy carrying crate, prepared to claim Foo-Foo, Piggy started by toying with him. She said, "Is your name Bono?"

"No."

"Is your name Ludacris?"

"No."

"What about Zayn?"

"Uh-uh."

"Then perhaps your name is . . . Unclestiltskin?"

The creature's blue face turned crimson with fury. "Who told you that?!" he fumed. *"Who has told you that!"* He was so mad that he plunged his right foot through the floor and his whole leg followed, and then in rage he pulled at his left leg so hard with both hands that he literally ripped himself in two.

Jacques shook his head in disgust. "That was so totally gross."

Piggy nodded. "But it sure confirms something *moi* always suspected about that guy: most extreme case of split personality ever!"

Bella Thorn, the Sleeping Beauty
(Not the Actress)

AFTER "BRIAR-ROSE"

O nce upon a time there was a king and queen by the names of Big Mean Carl and Mean Mama. Both had an uncommon mixture of royal and monster blood, but their longings were universal. They said every day, "Ah, if only we had a child!" But they never got one. They figured the storks must be on strike.

Mean Mama was a ravenous rabbit-bear hybrid who'd turned to food to fill the void, compulsively consuming everything in sight. One day she left the castle to avoid the kitchen and was taking a melancholy stroll by the seashore.

There's no two ways about it: She was very scary. How scary? When the tide came in and saw her, it screamed, went out again, and didn't come back.

As the sun reached its highest point in the sky, a mottled fish the color of an overripe avocado finned itself out of the water onto the land and said to her:

"Greetings from this guy, magic Walleye Pike,
Bringing ya some baby news I think you're gonna like:
Within one year you'll have yourself a daughter.
Ouch—I gotta split 'fore this sand gets any hotter!"

Before he could go, Mean Mama, overjoyed, grabbed him and opened her maw. Walleye exclaimed, "Hey, don't eat the messenger!" but it was too late: He was suddenly sushi.

What the unfortunate but delicious fish proclaimed did indeed come true: Nine months later the queen had a little rat, and named her Yolanda. The king, with his gray fur, softball-size yellow eyes, and bovine horns, lit up with joy. "Call the caterers!" he commanded, and he ordered a great feast. The finest pepperoni pizza and chicken tenders were to be served on 24-karat gold plates, with three-scoop rocky road floats as dessert for all. He arranged to have the Gogolala Jubilee Jugband perform, with an acrobatic interlude by the Flying Zucchini Brothers. And seated in a place of honor would be the kingdom's thirteen revered Wise Chickens, so that they might be kind and well-disposed toward the newborn rodent.

There was just one little hitch in an otherwise awesome event: The caterers showed up one place setting short. So while twelve of the Wise Chickens were able to join in the merriment, one of them was left out.

When the shindig came to an end, as was the custom, the Wise Chickens each bestowed their magic gifts upon baby Yolanda, who was swaddled inside a bread basket. One gave virtue, another looks, a third the sharpest of incisors, and so on, with everything in the world that one rat could wish for.

When eleven of them had made their promises, suddenly the excluded thirteenth stormed into the banquet hall. This chicken was named Camilla, and she was roasting with rage, bent on getting even with those who snubbed her. She'd racked her bird brain for the best curse with which to smite them, and she'd devised a doozy.

Without greeting or looking at anyone, Camilla put them on blast, flapping her wings and addressing Big Mean Carl and Mean Mama: *"Cluck cluck bawk b'gark ba-kawwww!"* Then she dug the claws of her right foot into the floor and used her left to spin herself around, and out the door she strode.

The big mean king looked about, bewildered. "Uh," he said to the crowd, "does anybody speak chicken?" The royal-court reporter, pink-complected Zelda Rose— who had conveniently been sitting to the side of the proceedings all night with her stenotype machine taking shorthand of the proceedings—lifted her glasses from her long, incongruously orange nose and read back from the transcript in a tremulous voice: "The king's daughter shall in her fifteenth year prick herself with a spindle, and fall down dead."

Everyone was stunned speechless—that is, all but the twelfth Wise Chicken, whose good wish still remained unspoken. She shuffled forward, and while everyone knew she could not *undo* the evil sentence, they hoped she could somehow soften it. This chick took a deep breath, cleared her craw, and pronounced, *"Bgark bawk bawk cluck bawk b'gawk."*

The king shrugged, uncomprehending, and looked to Zelda, who read back the translation: "It shall not be death but a deep sleep of a hundred years into which the princess shall fall."

Instantly, Big Mean Carl's characteristic orneriness returned. The king, who would fain keep his dear darling rodent from the misfortune thrust in her direction, issued an edict: "From henceforth, every spindle in the whole kingdom must be burned!" As the hoi polloi erupted in a hubbub, Carl could be heard asking Mama, "What the heck is a spindle, anyway?"

Meanwhile, the gifts of the Wise Chickens were plenteously fulfilled as young Yolanda grew up, for she turned out to be modest, good-natured, and an excellent gnawer, and everyone who saw her was bound to fall for her.

It happened that on the very day when Yolanda turned fifteen years old, the king and queen were away from home picking up her quinceañera tiara. The young rat was left in the palace quite alone, and she went sniffing around into all sorts of places, looking into rooms and bed chambers just as she liked, till at last she came to an old tower she'd never explored. "I probably oughta be cautious, since this is just the kinda thing that leads to trouble," she muttered. "Ah, on second thought, to heck with it."

She made her way up the narrow winding staircase and finally reached a little wooden door. A rusty key was in the lock, and when she turned it, the door sprang open—there in a little room sat a chicken with a spindle, wearing a curious expression and busily spinning her flax.

"Hiya, chick," said Yolanda. "What's doin'? What sort of thing is that, rattlin' around so funny? Can I give it a go?" The chicken scooted aside, offering her stool to the rat. But scarcely had Yolanda touched the spindle when the magic decree was fulfilled, and she pricked her finger on it, exclaiming, "Heavens to Betsy!" The chicken, who you might have by now deduced was Camilla, let loose a creepy cackle and disappeared. And, in the very moment when Yolanda felt the prick, she keeled over upon a bed conveniently placed right beside the spinning wheel and fell into a deep slumber.

This cursed sleeping sickness immediately spread over the whole palace. Big Mean Carl and Mean Mama, who had just come home, dropped off in a doze in the great hall, and the whole of the court along with them: Their horse Paul Revere went to sleep in the stable, their pooch Muppy in the yard, Fletcher Bird upon the roof, a coterie of prairie dogs in the field; even the fire that was flaming on the hearth stopped midflicker, so completely frozen it actually hummed "Let It Go." In the kitchen, the Swedish Chef yawned and uttered, "Uh-øh, goeen tu snøøzy stad." The lemon soufflé cooling on the counter suddenly became a sweet pillow for his Nordic noggin.

In the period that followed, all around the castle there began to grow a hedge of thorns that every year became higher, and soon it covered the walls and roofs so that there was nothing of the fortress to be seen, not even the satellite dish upon the roof.

But the story of the beautiful sleeping "Bella Thorn"— as the princess was nicknamed because, y'know, she was pretty and because, y'know, the thorns—made its way around the kingdom, so that from time to time suitors who thought she was the former star of *Shake It Up* came and tried to get through the perilously prickly hedge into the castle. But they were spared the disappointment of finding not a starlet but a sleeping rat because the thorns held fast together, and the unsuspecting stans got trapped in them and couldn't get loose. When consulted, the town doctor, Julius Strangepork, gave the cause of death as "sticker shock."

After many, many years, a tough-talking, style-conscious rat named Rizzo came to town from New York to visit Vests 'N' Jests, a specialty waistcoat store/comedy club owned by local joker and former ferry operator Fozzie Bear. While trying on various styles, Rizzo said, "So I saw that overgrown eyesore in the middle'a town— big three-story, block-long clump of thornbush? What gives?"

Fozzie nodded. "Yeah, underneath all that is Mean's Castle. Inside there's supposed to be a beautiful princess who's been asleep for many, many years, name of Bella Thorn. Not the actress. And the whole rest of the court is said to be sleeping, too. We're always getting these guys who try to hack through the thorny hedge to rescue the princess, but they get stuck in there and die a prickly death."

Rizzo laughed. "Amateurs! I ain't afraid. I'll go get

this beautiful Bella Thorn, Not the Actress, and mark my word, we'll get hitched."

Fozzie nodded. "You wear that handsome vest and it's sure to seal the deal."

Rizzo paid up and beelined to the castle. Unbeknownst to him, the hundred years had just passed and it was the exact day when Yolanda was prophesied to awake again. As he approached the imposing briar, it turned into nothing but large and beautiful flowers, which parted and let him pass unhurt. "What'd I tell ya," he said to the silence. "Rizzo is invincible!"

In the stable he noticed the horse and in the yard the hound, both fast asleep; on the roof sat the bird with his head under his wing. Rizzo went into the great hall and saw the whole of the court in its ceaseless nap, and up by the throne lay Big Mean Carl and Mean Mama, spooning. In the kitchen, the Swedish Chef still snøøzed on the remains of the soufflé.

Rizzo searched still farther and at last he climbed the tower and opened the door into the little room. There lay Yolanda, so beautiful in her sleep that he could not turn his little rat eyes away. He stooped down and gave her snout a kiss.

Yolanda awoke and looked at him quite sweetly. "Hey, nice vest," she said and yawned.

After they went downstairs together, Carl awoke, then Mean Mama, and finally the whole court, and they all looked at each other in great astonishment. Paul Revere stood and shook out his mane; Muppy jumped up and wagged his tail; Fletcher Bird upon the roof pulled his head out from under his wing.

And the Swedish Chef immediately began preparations for the joyous wedding of Rizzo and Yolanda—first and foremost making sure that there would be enough place settings for all who wanted to attend.

Clueless Trades a Turtle

AFTER "LAZY HEINZ"

Clueless Morgan was a supremely lazy goat. His motto was: "If at first you don't succeed, failure may be your thing."

Although he had nothing else to do but take his pet turtle out to the pasture every day, he nevertheless grumbled each evening when he returned home from the chore. "Taking care of a turtle is in truth a heavy burden and a tiresome job," mused the gap-toothed ruminant. "Shooing the turtle out to the lettuce patch day in and day out . . . if I could only lie down and sleep while doing it! But no, I must keep my eyes open so it doesn't run away. Turtles are so fast . . ."

Clueless sat down, collected his thoughts, and considered how he could ease this burden. Suddenly he got a brainstorm. "My head is so smart! I now know what I will do! I will marry my neighbor Dorothy Bovine, an attractive-enough cow. She, too, has a turtle, and she can

189

take mine out with hers, and then I shall no longer have to torment myself. If only she didn't live so far away."

Clueless slowly got up, set his four weary limbs into motion, and clip-clopped across the street, for it was no farther than that to where Dorothy Bovine lived with her parents. There, he asked them for permission to wed their cud-chewing offspring with her admirable four-chambered stomach. Her parents couldn't say yes fast enough, desperate as they were to get their dim daughter out the door. They knew all too well that if her IQ was any lower, she'd trip over it.

So Dorothy became Clueless's wife, and daily managed the care and feeding of both of the turtles. She also started an Instagram account for the pet pair and filled it with what she termed "shellfies."

Lazy Clueless now enjoyed doing nothing to the fullest, having no work to rest from. But, in truth, Dorothy was no less lazy. She was the type that'd stand with a bottle of ketchup and wait for an earthquake.

"Dear Clueless," Dorothy said one afternoon, "why should we make our lives so miserable, ruining the best days of our youth, when there is no need for it? Those two turtles disturb our best sleep every morning with their inaudible movements and inconvenient need to eat. Wouldn't it be better for us to offer them to our beekeeping neighbor, Animal, who could trade us a hive in exchange? We can put the hive in a sunny place behind the house and then not give it any more thought. Bees don't have to be taken care of, or fed, or promoted on social media. They fly out and find their way home again by themselves, and they make delicious honey without any effort at all on our part."

"You have spoken like a sensible cow," replied Clueless. "We will carry out your plan without delay so that we may do even less with our days."

They called Animal with their proposal and he said he would be overjoyed to trade a beehive for the two reptiles. The neighborhood wild man greeted the goat and the cow enthusiastically at his front door with two words: *"Tuuuuurtle souuuuuuuup!"*

Dorothy stopped in her tracks. "Did he say 'turtle soup'? He's not going to *eat* them, is he?"

"No, I think he was just naming them," Clueless said confidently. "As in, Turtle Sue. I wonder what he'll name the other."

"Meeeeal, meeeeal!"

"Okay, sure." Clueless nodded. "Neil is a fine name."

Animal took the turtles and headed straight for his kitchen.

Returning to their house, Clueless and Dorothy

placed the new hive in their backyard. The bees flew in and out of the box from early morning until late evening, filling it with the best honey. By autumn, Clueless took out a whole jugful, which they stored on a shelf on their bedroom wall, fearing that it might be stolen otherwise. Dorothy even bought an aluminum baseball bat and put it beside the bed. Her plan going forward was to get out of bed as little as possible. She would be able to reach the bat without having to get up, and drive away any would-be honey thieves. Clueless agreed that staying in bed all the time was the best course of inaction. "Never put off until tomorrow," he said, "what you can put off until the day after tomorrow."

Dorothy chucked the goat affectionately on the chin. "You said it, kid."

One morning when he was still lying in bed in broad daylight, recovering from his exhausting fourteen-hour slumber, Clueless said to his wife, "Fess up: You're too fond of sweets, and you have been snacking on the honey when I'm not looking, haven't you?"

The cow got sheepish.

Her hubby continued: "If you keep that up, it's going to be gone by the new year. Maybe it would be better for us to exchange it for a goose and a young gosling."

"Without a child to do the work?" replied Dorothy,

with a sassy swivel of her neck. "Am I to torment myself chasing after young geese, wasting all my energy on them for no reason?"

"Do you think," said Clueless, "that a child would even tend geese? Nowadays children no longer obey. They do just as they please, because they think that they are smarter than their parents."

"Oh, our child will get an earful if he doesn't do what I say. I will take this bat and—"

"Wife!" Clueless interrupted her, appalled. "Surely you wouldn't harm our child?!"

"Husband, chill. I was going to say, I will take this bat and hide it from him as punishment, and he won't be able to play baseball. That'll make him listen." She pretended to be a batter eyeing a pitch and swung the bat at the imaginary ball—but she only hit the jug of honey above the bed and cracked it. The sticky liquid dripped down and puddled on them and on the bedsheets. Clueless and Dorothy both tried to avoid making eye contact, hoping the other would be the first to address the mess. Neither did.

"Whew," said Dorothy, "I'm too exhausted from swinging the bat to do anything."

"And I'm so tired, I have an itch on my leg I'm six months behind on scratching."

"I can't even find the energy to sleep walk—I have to sleep hitchhike."

After a while Clueless noticed that there was still some honey at the bottom of the broken jug that lay right between them on the bed. "Wife, let us enjoy the leftovers, and then we will rest a little from the fright we've had."

"If only the jug didn't require me to sit up and reach for it," Dorothy lamented.

But her husband didn't hear her. He was already fast asleep.

The Frog Who Liked to Fish

AFTER "THE FISHERMAN AND HIS WIFE"

There was once a frog who liked to fish. His name was Kermit, and he lived off the grid with his wife, Piggy, in a humble ditch by the sea.

One day after walking to the nearby shore, the green guy cast his line into the water and sat looking at the sparkling waves. He soon felt a tug and saw the bobber start bobbing. He reeled in the line and up came a great big fish—or maybe it wasn't *fully* a fish, because it had a rather unique appearance. For starters, it wore sunglasses. And instead of scales, it had soft, spongy lilac flesh and sprouts of patchy goatee in shades of fuchsia and purple. On its head was a tangle of long, similarly shaded dreadlocks.

This odd catch held out its two arms, and pleaded, "Hey there, my name's Clifford and I'm not a real fish. I'm an enchanted prince is what I am. Whatta ya say you put me back in the water?"

"Hi ho!" called Kermit, who then gently removed the lure from the creature's gills. "You don't need to convince me, Clifford. From one talking aquatic creature to another, I'd never want to see you come to any harm. Off you go!" Clifford saluted him, dived into a cresting wave, and disappeared out of sight.

When Kermit returned to the ditch, he told Piggy how he had caught the massive fish-being, and how it claimed to be an enchanted prince, and how, after he heard it speak, he had let it go again.

"Excusez-moi?" said Piggy, planting a fist on each hip, her volume increasing incrementally. "You captured an enchanted prince, and then *let him go*—WITHOUT ASKING FOR ANYTHING IN RETURN?!"

Kermit shook his head, dazed. "Now I know why they call them eardrums. Mine just took a beating."

She poked a finger into his chest. "Does it not bother you that we live wretchedly here in this nasty, dirty ditch? Oh sure, at least we have running water—running right through everything anytime it rains! Do you know how embarrassing it is for me when we have company over? Do you not remember the look Yolanda Rat gave Rizzo when she asked where the bathroom was and you laughed and said, 'Where *isn't* it?'"

"Ah, come on, that was pretty funny." But she

remained stern. "Don't worry, Piggy, we'll move up from here," he gingerly offered, knowing that was the wrong thing to say. When she was perturbed like this, there wasn't a *right* thing to say. "We just need to give it some time?"

"If you think things improve with time, Kermit, you oughta go to a class reunion. Now, you will march right back to the sea and tell that talking fish that we want a big fat mansion. Something so big we'll have to shampoo the carpets with a crop duster!"

The humble frog did not much like all this business, but he finally consented to return to the seashore as she asked. When he got to the ocean, he stood at the water's edge, and said:

> *"Clifford, Clifford, prince of the sea!*
> *Please hear this call and come to me.*
> *If asking a favor isn't too much of a biggie,*
> *I'll pass along a request from my wife, Piggy."*

Clifford suddenly surfaced, swam to him, and said, "Well, what's the ol' ball-and-chain want?"

"Er," said Kermit, wringing his hands, "she says that when I caught you I ought to have asked you for something before I let you go. See, Piggy says she doesn't like living in a ditch, and wants . . ." Kermit swallowed hard. "A big fat mansion?"

The waves broke and frothed around the fish-thing's feet as he contemplated. "All right, look," he finally said, "you didn't have to release me, but you did, so you can consider Clifford your homey in the foamy. Go on back—she's in the mansion already!"

When Kermit returned, he was amazed to find, standing in place of the ditch, a huge home and estate. Piggy was doing a happy dance in the doorway, giddily waving to him. "Didn't I tell you?!"

"We have so many rooms," he marveled while touring the house. "A cloakroom, a foyer, a billiards room, a larder, a conservatory. And I don't even know what a conservatory *is*." Then he snapped his fingers. "Piggy! After dinner why don't we have dessert in the study."

"We can't. The librarians lock it up at six."

"Oh well, tomorrow then. How happy we'll be now!"

"Well, we'll try at least," said the pig, a note of uncertainty in her voice.

Everything went right for a week or two, till one morning Piggy cooed, "Kermie, we have all these shelves in the house and nothing to display on them. What if Yolanda and Rizzo come over again? You know how judge-y they are. I would like to have a little something to display. To, you know, *show off*. Like maybe an *award*."

Kermit's eyes narrowed. "An award?"

"Yes, an award. Like, say, the Newbery Medal."

"The one that goes to excellence in children's literature?" he asked, incredulous. "Um, have you *read* this book we're in? Neeeever gonna happen."

"Fine, then how about an *Emmy*?"

"Piggy, the Muppets have already won Emmys."

"But not for *moi* personally. And I've got an empty trophy case just waiting for that glorious golden statuette! Surely you can see how unjust it all is. Go to the fish again and tell him to give *moi* one little Emmy."

"I don't feel right about this. He might get mad. We ought to just be happy with this amazing mansion."

"Poppycock!" said Piggy. "We have an opportunity here, Kerm. We can't give up now—imagine if a particular scientist had given up when he only got to Preparation G!"

So Kermit went, but his heart was very heavy. When he came to the sea, it looked calm and blue, but a bit gloomy. He inched close to the edge of the surf, and said:

"Clifford, Clifford, prince of the sea!
Please hear this call and come to me.
If asking a favor isn't too much of a biggie,
I'll pass along a request from my wife, Piggy."

"Well, what does she want now?" said the enchanted prince when he surfaced.

"Ah!" replied the doleful frog. "This time my wife wants . . . an Emmy Award."

"Go back to your mansion, then," said Clifford. "She's got it in her hot little hands already."

So away went Kermit, and when he got home, he found Piggy standing before the mirror holding her statuette and giving her acceptance speech. "For *moi*? *Quelle surprise!* I'm so humbled. I'd like to thank my agent, my manager, my attorney, my voice coach, my herbalist, my Reiki master, and, most of all, *moi*self.

"Congratulations," said Kermit. "You're an Emmy winner, and now we can live luxuriously in this beautiful mansion for the rest of our lives."

"Perhaps," she replied halfheartedly, "but let's sleep on it before we make up our minds."

The next morning Piggy woke him with an urgent shake. "Kermie! I need something else. The Emmy is nice and all, but you know what would *really* make me happy? A Grammy Award."

"But the Muppets have won two Grammys already." He saw her face contort and realized what she was about to say. "Right, yes, but not for you personally, no."

"Kermie," said she, "don't you think I deserve my own?"

"It's not so much a question of deserving, as it is a question of . . . Well, no, it is a question of deserv—"

"Go and try!" she implored. Then she softened, changing tack. "Think about it: The inventor in charge of concocting soda formulas would have never forgiven himself if he'd stopped at 6 Up!"

So the frog went away quite heavyhearted to think that his wife should want so much. This time the sea looked a dark gray color, and was crisscrossed with curling waves and ridges of foam as he cried out:

"Clifford, Clifford, prince of the sea!
Please hear this call and come to me.
If asking a favor isn't too much of a biggie,
I'll pass along a request from my wife, Piggy."

"Well, what would she have now?" said Clifford when he surfaced.

"Oh dear!" said poor Kermit. "Piggy wants her own Grammy Award."

"No sweat," he replied. "She's holding it already."

Then Kermit went home, and as he entered the mansion he saw Piggy with her Grammy trophy, giving an acceptance speech in front of the mirror. ". . . my trainer, my nutritionist, my back scratcher, but most of all, *moi*self."

"Well, Piggy," said Kermit, "please tell me you are happy now?"

"Well, *duh*," said she. "Everyone knows happiness comes solely from external validation."

"And now we'll never have anything more to wish for as long as we live . . . right?"

"Oh puh-leeze. Never is a long time. I am an Emmy winner, and a Grammy winner, sure. But . . . I wouldn't want those two trophies to be lonely on the shelf. Three's company, *oui*? What if they had a little friend named . . . Oscar?"

"You mean—an Academy Award?!"

"You think I'd settle for a SAG Award? Go to the fish and get *moi* one little Oscar! At least ask!"

Kermit complained to himself as he walked to the seashore, "This will come to no good. It's too much to ask. Clifford will be sick of it, and then we'll be sorry for what we've done." He soon arrived to find the water quite black and muddy. A mighty whirlwind blew over the waves and rolled them about, but he inched as near as he dared to the water's brink, and said:

"Clifford, Clifford, prince of the sea!
Please hear this call and come to me.
If asking a favor isn't too much of a biggie,

204

I'll pass along a request from my wife, Piggy."

"What does the sow want now?" said Clifford.

"Well . . . ," said Kermit sheepishly, "she wants an Oscar."

"Go on home—it's already in her hands."

"Wow, you are strangely agreeable."

"Yeah, things are good, my man. I've been seeing a mermaid and I'm pretty excited. Tonight's our fifth date."

"So it's getting serious?"

Clifford nodded. "Yep, I think she might be gill-friend material."

Kermit went home again and found Piggy in front of the mirror, holding her statuette: ". . . my ear candler, my pigskin rejuvenator, my cryogenic-chamber attendant, but most of all, *moi*self."

Kermit asked, "Are you happy now?"

"Yes," said she, "I am an Oscar winner! But . . . I really want to EGOT."

"What's EGOT?"

"An EGOTer is someone who wins an Emmy, a Grammy, an Oscar, and the coveted Tony Award for their work on Broadway. Like Mel Brooks, Rita Moreno, Marvin Hamlisch, and Whoopi Goldberg. They're EGOTers. I mean, why should I stop now when I'm just one win away from joining those legends?"

"Are you really going to make me go and ask him . . . ?" That was a rhetorical question. [Editor's Note: What do you get when you cross a joke with a rhetorical question?]

While the reader pondered that one, the frog went to the shore and found the wind raging and the sea tossing up and down in boiling waves, and the ships in trouble upon the tops of the billows. And the sky became black with storm clouds as a storm arose, so that the trees and the very rocks shook. At this sight, Kermit was dreadfully frightened, and he trembled so much that his skinny little frog knees knocked together. But still he said:

"Clifford, Clifford, prince of the sea!
Please hear this call and come to me.
If asking a favor isn't too much of a biggie,
I'll pass along a request from my wife, Piggy."

"What does she want now?" said the enchanted prince.

"Clifford, I'm so sorry to ask," said Kermit, "but my wife wants to win a Tony."

"A *Tony*?!" Lightning flashed and thunder cracked. Clifford recoiled. "Win a Tony without paying her dues?

Who does she think she is, disrespecting Broadway?! Go home," he said, monumentally irked. "She's back in the ditch!"

And so she was, and there they live to this very day.

Pepé and Polly

AFTER "HANSEL AND GRETEL"

In a modest condo on the edge of a great forest dwelt a retired woodcutter named Statler. He lived there with his lifelong pal, roommate, and verbal sparring partner, Waldorf. They believed that hurling an insult a day kept the doctor away.

The duo shared their household with two oceanic offspring, Pepé the King Prawn and Polly Lobster. Since Statler had thrown out his back and been unable to return to his logging job at Grimm Timber Industries, they had very little to eat. His disability checks barely even covered their daily bread.

As for Waldorf, he didn't work at all. He didn't feel like it. "You're so lazy," Statler would often gripe. "If opportunity knocked you'd sit back and complain about the noise." But it didn't change anything.

One night when Statler was thinking over their dire financial situation in bed, tossing about in anxiety, he finally gave up on sleep and padded into Waldorf's room to wake him. Statler gave him a good shake and said, "I can't figure out how we're supposed to feed those crustaceans when we can barely even feed ourselves."

"Well . . . ," began his groggy friend, "I didn't want to say anything, but now that you bring it up . . . if we boiled a big pot of water, those two would make a delicious—"

"Stop right there. We're not eating our kids. This isn't *Game of Thrones*. Which we've never seen because we can't afford HBO. And anyway, I thought you were allergic to seafood."

"It's not an allergy, it's a preference. The only seafood I like is saltwater taffy."

Statler exhaled, exasperated. "We need a plan here, Waldorf, not a sharing circle."

"Fine, here's the plan: Early tomorrow morning we take the two out into the forest to where it's the thickest."

"But you hate Mother Nature."

"Only because she makes mornings come so early." He yawned. "Besides, we won't stay in the woods long. We just light a campfire, we give them peanut butter and plankton sandwiches, and then we split."

Statler was taken aback. "You mean, just *leave* them there?"

"They won't be able to find the way home again, and,

voilà, we'll be rid of them. We won't even miss them. Seriously, they might as well become astronauts."

"Why's that?"

"They just sit at home taking up space!" Waldorf threw off the covers and sat up. "I mean, they're not even good students. In school, Pepé misbehaves like crazy. He gets paddled more than a canoe. And Polly is so dim he'd look for a wishbone in a hard-boiled egg."

"I dunno. He kinda grows on you."

"So do warts."

Statler turned on the bedside lamp and rubbed his temples. "If we abandon them out in the forest, the wild animals would soon come and mistake them for a raw bar."

"Oh, you sentimental old fool!" said Waldorf. "If we *don't* do this, we'll all four go hungry."

"But I couldn't live with myself."

"Trust me: If *I* can manage to live with you all these years, you'll figure it out."

In the next room, Pepé and Polly had also not been able to sleep—their very vocal empty stomachs had growled them awake (and lobsters have *two* stomachs, so it was double loud for Polly). While lying there, they'd overheard what Waldorf had proposed. Polly wrapped all his legs around himself in a self-pitying hug and whispered morosely, "Well, that's the end of us, ain't no doubt about it."

"Not so fast, okay," countered Pepé, who knew all too well of Polly's tendency to prematurely throw in the towel. "You are such the pessimist."

"Look, Pepé, it's just that I know life is like a car wash. And me?" He shrugged. "I'm goin' through it on a bike."

"We will find the way out of this, okay," Pepé said, patting his pal's one and only claw. "Leave it to me."

"You see the glass half full. I see it half empty. Either way, you wind up with a dirty glass."

When the determined prawn finally heard the old men snoring again, he got up and pulled on his track suit, then silently opened the front door and stole outside. The moon was nearly full and lit up the white pebbles that lay among the condo building's landscaping so that they shone like silver coins. Pepé stuffed the pockets of his jacket with as many as he could fit. Then he went back in and lay down again in his bed, plenty pleased.

When day dawned, Waldorf popped his bald pate into their room and barked, "Get up, you sluggards! We're going into the forest to fetch wood."

The prawn tittered. "You?! *You* are going walking?"

"Don't look so surprised. I'm in great shape."

"Yeah," Statler piped up from down the hall. "There's

only one thing harder than his muscles—his arteries!"

Waldorf handed Pepé and Polly each half a sandwich in a Ziploc. "Here's something for lunch, but don't eat it before then, because you won't be getting anything else." Then they all set out together into the forest. But instead of taking the well-used path, the fogies forged another route that was altogether unfamiliar to Pepé and Polly, who followed warily.

When they had walked a short time, the prawn paused and peered back at the house. Then he did it again a moment later, and then again.

"Pepé, pay attention," said Statler, noticing his odd behavior. "Have you forgotten how to walk?"

"Is true, I am naturally a much better swimmer. I know all the strokes."

"I only know one kind of stroke," said Waldorf. "If you put me in the water and make me exercise, I have one!"

Statler shushed them. "Can we please not talk about strokes? I don't need any reminders that I'm getting older. Every day I look in the mirror and I see that my cheeks are hollow, my skin is sallow, my whiskers are white, and my hair is falling out."

"Cheer up," Waldorf offered, "at least you still have twenty-twenty vision!"

This got them both laughing, till they noticed Pepé pausing again. Waldorf asked, "Why are you lagging behind now?"

"I am looking at my leetle dog, Timex. He is sitting at the edge of the wood, okay, and he want to say *adios* to me."

Statler was puzzled. "Why would you name him Timex?"

"Because he is a watch dog, okay."

Waldorf scoffed. "That is *not* your dog—who would trust you with a pet, anyway? You couldn't even keep your Tamagotchi alive."

When they had reached the middle of the forest, Statler said, "Now, the two of you go and pile up some wood and I'll light a fire so you won't be cold." Pepé and Polly gathered a little hill of brush and twigs. Statler threw a match onto it, and when the flames were burning high, Waldorf said, "Now, you guys just hang out here and do nothing. I know for a fact that's something you're good at!" He chortled. "We'll go into the forest to chop some wood."

Pepé raised an eyebrow. "Oh, is that so? I thought Statler couldn't chop woods anymore because of his back."

"He can't," said Waldorf, scowling. "Which is . . . why *I'm* going to do the chopping."

"But you didn't bring an ax," said Polly.

"I, uh, stashed an ax in the wood last time I was here."

"The last time?" said Pepé. "I thought you hated going into the woods, okay."

Waldorf replied, "I know you are but what am I!"

Pepé looked askance at him.

"I'm rubber and you're glue," Waldorf tried again, floundering.

"You are not very good with the comebacks, okay."

At a loss, Waldorf blurted, "Infinity!" and off the two old men went.

Pepé and Polly got themselves comfortable by the fire. When noon came, each ate his sandwich. Since they could hear the strokes of an ax not too far away, they believed that Statler and Waldorf were still near and must be doing as they said they would.

After sitting for such a long time, their eyes closed from boredom. When at last their growling stomachs awakened them, it was already dark. They investigated the chopping sound and discovered with dismay that it was a branch Waldorf had fastened to a withered tree; the wind was blowing it back and forth, knocking it against another tree's trunk.

"This is the exact reason I carry a card in my wallet that reads, IN CASE OF ACCIDENT, I'M NOT SURPRISED," whined the lobster. "Oh man, I'm so hungry." Predictably, he wanted a cracker. Polly always wanted a cracker.

"As soon as the moon goes up, we will be able to find the way out of the forest."

"Yeah, but how?"

"Hold your horse, okay, and you will see."

When the full moon had finally risen, Pepé took Polly by the claw, and together they followed the pebbles he had slipped out of his pocket and dropped along the path. "So *that's* why you kept stopping while we walked," said Polly, impressed.

After they walked a bit more, the prawn broke the silence. "You know, I've always wanted to ask how you lose your other claw, okay."

"It was an accident. I was a contestant on *The Price Is Right*. I gave the Big Wheel a spin, and off came the claw. I did make it to the Showcase Showdown," he said as he looked forlornly at his stump, "but the ultimate price was clearly not right."

They continued to backtrack from pebble to pebble the whole night long, and by the break of day, they came once more to the condo and knocked at the apartment door. When Waldorf opened it, he staggered back a step or two, then quickly regained his composure and chided them. "You naughty boys, why did you sleep so long in the forest? We thought you were never coming back!"

"The sad sadness must have been overwhelming," deadpanned Pepé. "I hope you are okay, okay."

Statler, for his part, was secretly happy to see them. However curmudgeonly he may have generally appeared, leaving them behind in the woods had certainly plucked the one heartstring he had left.

A few nights after their return, Pepé and Polly overheard Waldorf complain to Statler, "Everything is eaten again. We have only one box of Bagel Bites and some saltines left, and that is the end. No joke. Those two freeloading sea insects must go. This time we'll take them farther into the wood—so far that they won't find their way out." Statler tried to argue, but Waldorf wouldn't listen. He *couldn't* listen: He had deliberately taken out his hearing aid.

When the old folks were finally asleep, Pepé again got up to go and gather pebbles, as he had done before, but Waldorf had locked the front door and kept the key!

"Oh great," moaned Polly, "that's the end of us."

"That is the wrong attitudes! Is just a teeny tiny setback. Are we going to let that stop us?"

The lobster shrugged. "Yes?"

"Guess again."

"No?"

"That's the spirits! Now Pepé will come up with the plan."

Early in the morning, Waldorf rousted them from their beds. He gave them each a single cracker for lunch. Such a meager portion would be mortifying to most, but Polly was delighted regardless. He couldn't wait till noon and gobbled his down immediately. On the way into the forest, however, Pepé secretly crumbled his cracker in his pocket, and often paused to throw a white crumb on the black dirt.

On they walked, and little by little, Pepé threw all the morsels onto the ground as Waldorf led them still deeper into the forest, where they had never in their lives been before. Then a great fire was again made, and Waldorf said, "We'll go into the forest to chop some wood, and when we're finished, we'll come back and fetch you."

"Yeahhhh," said Polly, "I think I've heard this story before . . ."

They waited till Statler and Waldorf had gotten some distance away, then Pepé said, "Now we outsmart them, okay, and follow the crumbs back home." And for a time, the plan worked—at least until they ran into a big, bald, blue bird lurching in their direction. He was pecking at the ground every couple of paces, scarfing down all the cracker bits that Pepé had left to mark the trail!

"Hey, wingnut," called Polly, "whatta ya think you're doin' there?"

"I am enjoying the abundant bounty of America's pristine forests."

"Oh yeah?" said Polly. "And where do you think that bounty came from? A saltine tree? You've eaten so many crumbs, if you were a chicken you'd be laying a roll!"

"I am no chicken, thank you very much," said the bird, ruffling its feathers. "I'll have you know I am Sam Eagle. I am the patriotic symbol of this great country and a firm believer in the right of an individual in a democratic society to avail him- or herself of the land's natural resources, so long as one is respectful of said resources. I'm merely snacking on freely found food and doing no harm. And now I am full, so I shall say 'harrumph' and 'good day' to you both!" And with that, he flew away.

Their path home now erased, they walked the whole night and all the next day, from morning till evening, but they did not get out of the forest. They were very hungry, for they had nothing to eat but two or three late-blooming crunch berries, which they found on a half-dead Cap'n Crunch bush. At one point, they stumbled upon a vending machine stocked with Kit Kat bars, but alas, they had no money. "Gimme a break," groaned Polly.

Soon, they were so weary that their legs could carry them no longer, and they lay down beneath a tree and fell asleep. When it was dawn, they began to walk again, but they always somehow went deeper into the forest. It had now been three days since they'd left the condo, and Pepé was now even feeling nostalgic for its old-people smell.

When it was midday, they heard a great flapping ruckus from above, and suddenly Sam Eagle swooped down through the treetops and alighted on a branch just in front of them. "There you are!" he exclaimed. "I've been looking for you for days. I felt it was my duty as a fellow American and an Eagle Scout in good standing to let you know that I think I spotted your house just over that hill. Funny, I've never seen it in all my time living in these woods. And I've certainly never before seen a house made of candy and cakes and crackers."

Pepé thanked Sam. "That is not our house, okay, but we will be happy for the shelters."

"And the crackers!" said Polly as he sprinted ahead.

The bird saluted and took wing. When Pepé reached the crest of the little hill, he did indeed see, incredibly, a quaint cottage built of crackers and covered with candy and cakes, its windows made of clear sugar. Polly was already nibbling on a saltine wall. Pepé joined him, pulling off a length of candy-cane trim just as the front door opened and a reptilian creature with short, curved horns, a long snout, and small, pointy teeth came creeping out. He wore a tattered, old-fashioned suit with a buttoned-up vest. His piercing green eyes glowed in deep black sockets, and his leathery skin was a powdery blue.

Pepé and Polly were so spooked that they immediately stopped their snacking and stepped back. "Wow," whispered Polly, "that thing's so ugly it could curdle a cow."

The homely homeowner tilted his head and gently held up a hand, its four fingers tipped with sharp claws, to calm the two. "Oh, you dear sea creatures, do not be afraid. Come in and sit for a spell with me. No harm shall come to you. My name is Uncle Deadly."

"'Deadly'?" Polly looked at Pepé. "All right now, granted, I'm a pessimist, but something tells me this isn't a good—"

"You must be so hungry," purred Uncle Deadly. "I have all different kinds of crackers already set out on the table."

Polly bolted through the door before Pepé could blink. Now he had no choice but to follow.

Once inside, a bounty of delicious food was set before them, and so intoxicated by the aromas were they that reservations were put aside and they dug in.

When they had eaten their fill, Deadly led them to two beds covered with clean white linens. As they were quite exhausted from their ordeal in the woods, they lay down and immediately fell sound asleep.

The prehistoric thing remained standing over them, a dark grin spreading across his ghastly features.

As you've no doubt deduced, this Uncle Deadly was only pretending to be kind; in reality, he was a wicked warlock who lay in wait for prey, and had only conjured the little house of crackers and sweets in order to entice these particular prizes into his lair. When someone fell into his power—and here you should cover your eyes if you're easily frightened, although that might make reading a tad difficult—he killed them, cooked them, and ate them!

Early the next morning, Uncle Deadly seized the sleeping prawn by a leg and dropped him into a big glass bowl in the kitchen, covering the top with a heavy metal grating. Then Deadly went to Polly and said, "On your feet, lobster. It's time for you to whip up something fattening for the shrimp to eat. We're going to make him nice and plump so there will be more for me to savor when I put him into a gumbo and gobble him down!"

Polly rubbed his eyes and tried to comprehend, as the words he heard left him incredulous, shocked, and terrified: "I'm going to have to *cook*?!"

Uncle Deadly prodded him into the kitchen and barked instructions for getting the fire lit and the water boiling. At one point, when his captor was preoccupied, Polly dashed for the exit, but it was no use. Deadly had charmed the windows and doors to stay locked. There was no way to escape. Polly was forced to do what the wicked warlock commanded, and that meant toiling over the hot stove.

"Why are you so big on gumbo, anyway?" asked Polly. "You sound British, but gumbo's Cajun."

"Variety is the spice of life, my pet," said Uncle Deadly. "Just how much fried fish and chips do you think a limey can stomach?"

"How come I'm not going in the gumbo, too?"

"Oh, I don't like my lobster prepared like that," Uncle Deadly answered, somewhat ambiguously . . .

Polly conspired with Pepé every chance they got, but they couldn't think of a way out of their predicament—until one day, when they saw Uncle Deadly trying to walk through the door and he smacked headfirst into the wall. They realized that although warlocks have a keen sense of smell, their green eyes cannot see well at all. Which finally gave Pepé an idea.

Every morning Uncle Deadly slinked to the fishbowl,

and said, "Prawn, stretch out your tail so that I may feel if you have gotten fat enough." Clever Pepé, however, held out the candy cane he'd jammed into his pocket when Deadly first encountered them outside his house. Due to Deadly's dim warlock eyes, he thought he was feeling Pepé's tail and was astonished that no matter how much the prawn ate, there seemed to be no way of fattening him.

When four weeks had gone by and Pepé still remained thin, Uncle Deadly was seized with impatience and would not wait any longer. "Now then, Polly," he cried to the lobster, "bring some water for the cauldron. Whether Pepé's fat or lean, today I will kill him and you will cook him." Deadly tapped on the glass of Pepé's bowl and sang:

> *". . . you're certainly lucky you are, 'cause it's gonna be hot in my big silver pot. Tootle-loo, mon poisson, au revoir!"*

As the lobster prepped the cauldron with the water, chopped the okra, and made the roux from flour and fat, he racked his brain to figure out a way to avoid the seemingly inevitable fate awaiting his brother. But figuring out fixes was not his forte—Pepé had always made the plans.

"We will bake first," announced Deadly.

"Bake?" Polly turned around to face the blue brute. "What are we baking?"

"I have already heated the oven," said Deadly, conspicuously ignoring the question. He nudged poor Polly to the open oven door, from which flames were already darting.

"Go ahead," said Deadly, "see if it is properly heated." Of course, Polly realized that once his head was inside, Deadly intended to push in the rest of him and shut the oven. At that moment, he remembered how Deadly had said he didn't like lobster prepared in a gumbo—now it was clear that he preferred his lobster *broiled*!

"I uh . . . I don't know how to tell if it's properly heated," Polly stalled, scratching his head for dramatic effect. "How do you do that?"

"Oh, you nutter," said Uncle Deadly. "You just pop your head in."

"Pop your head in? What does that even mean?"

"How infuriating you are! You just stick it in like this." And as Deadly did what he described, Polly put his one claw to good use, giving the unsuspecting warlock a shove that sent him flying into the oven's maw. The lobster slammed the iron door and fastened the bolt, crowing, "And *that*, my blue-skinned friend, is what we call *closure*!" The lobster turned around and warmed his tush in the heat. Then he helped Pepé climb out of the fishbowl, and how they did rejoice and dance about!

As they had no longer any need to fear Uncle Deadly, they searched the house for anything that would help them get out of the forest and back home. What they found amazed them: chests full of pearls and jewels and gold! Pepé's eyes popped: "You know how the blings are my thing!" They thrust into their pockets everything that would fit, donned an array of chunky gold necklaces, and wrapped stone-encrusted bracelets around their wrists.

Deadly's door-locking charms were now disarmed, so away they fled. When they had traveled for nearly two hours (according to Pepé's fly new Rolex), they came to a rushing river that had no bridge. Swimming across was out of the question: Their haul would weigh them down and they'd sink to the bottom.

But just as Polly got morose and reached for his IN CASE OF ACCIDENT, I'M NOT SURPRISED card, Sam Eagle soared through an opening in the foliage overhead, landed next to them, and asked, "Did someone order a deus ex machina?"

Pepé was P.O.'d. "*You!* Did you know the house you send us to belonged to a warlock named Uncle Deadly who try to cook and eat us?"

"What?! I thought the only thing you had to worry about in this forest was *ticks*." Sam was astounded. "A warlock?! Why, that's positively unwholesome. How can I make it up to you?"

"How about you fly us over the river to the other side, okay," said Pepé.

"I can do better than that. Climb on my back." They did as he suggested, and he flew them high above the trees. ("Maybe too high?" squeaked freaked Polly through chattering teeth.) At length, Pepé pointed out the edge of the forest and soon spotted Statler and Waldorf's condo. Sam safely delivered them right to the doorstep.

Instead of heading for the old guys' apartment, Pepé led Polly to the building's rental office. There, using some of the warlock's jewels, the prawn struck a deal for their very own home, throwing in a diamond ring to ensure that they would be directly above Statler and Waldorf's place. And after they moved in, they stomped and jumped on the floor all day and night, creating such a ruckus that their downstairs neighbors never had any measure of peace and quiet.

"Well." Statler sighed. "At least there's *one* good thing about the racket from those rascals."

Waldorf was skeptical. "What's that?"

"It drowns out your snoring!"

They couldn't help but laugh. "Ho-hahahaha!"

Pepé and Polly, meanwhile, lived together above them in perfect happiness, with everything they could ever wish for, including a special cupboard stocked with crackers.

"Uh, hullooooo?" calls Uncle Deadly from the oven in his house deep in the forest. "*Anyone?* It's quite toasty in here." He knocks politely on the oven door. "You're not just going to leave me like this, surely?" He cups a hand to his ear, barely making out a boisterous hullabaloo in the distance. "People, do you not recall that I was the title character of the Muppets *Phantom of the Opera*?! This is no way to treat a *star*!"

But his appeal falls on deaf ears, as the rest of the book's Muppet players are already congratulating one another that they made it through the stories without any major disasters and can hear nothing above their own happy clamor.

"Wait!" cries Deadly. "This tale can't be over. You're kidding, right? . . . You're not kidding." He sighs. "Goodness gracious, is this *really* the end?"

And indeed, it really was the end.

Turns out they didn't call the brothers Grimm for nothing.

Epilogue

"Great job, everyone!" says Kermit to the cast and crew, who are buzzing on a post-performance high as they enjoy treats from the Swedish Chef's well-stocked craft services table.

At least that's the case till Scooter adds, "Don't pop the cork on that sparkling cider just yet—we've only got five minutes till we go again!"

Uncle Deadly, who has finally been freed from the oven and is grousing about his singed snout, stops in his tracks and turns back to the stage manager as the room suddenly silences. "I beg your pardon?" says Deadly. "'Go again'?"

Statler turns to Waldorf: "Did he say 'go again'?"

Waldorf turns to Statler, then turns up his hearing aid: "I'm pretty sure he did."

Scooter nods. "Yeah, see, like I told you before we started, that was our *dress rehearsal.* Now we have to perform it for real. Uh-oh . . . did I forget to tell you that before we started . . . ?"

The crowd erupts, some in excitement, some in panic. Feathers and fur fly.

"Relax, gang! It's just another chance to get it right," says Kermit, trying to calm the outcry. "Practice makes perfect!"

Pepé rolls his eyes. "*Sí, pero* if 'practice makes perfect,' and also if 'nobody's perfect,' then why practice at all?"

Janice nods. "Like, *deep*, man."

"Well," continues Kermit, "for a lot of us, it's not all about the end result. Getting there is half the fun."

"Half the fun?" says Waldorf. "That sounds *exactly* like what we've come to expect from the Muppets!"

But soon, excitement at the chance to give the stories another go takes over. The members of the Electric Mayhem begin tuning up their instruments. François Fromage wheels himself over to the refrigerator and stands in front of its open door, trying to stay chilled. Gonzo herds a flock of chickens back to their coops to await their entrances.

Inspired by the birds, Fozzie blurts out a new joke idea. "Hey, Gonzo! Why did the chicken cross the playground?"

"Gee, Foz, I dunno."

"To get to the other *slide*! Wocka wocka!"

"Good one! You should put that in one of your stories."

Meanwhile, the stagehand Beauregard trundles over to Kermit and Scooter. He wears once-white coveralls that are now Jackson Pollock'd with an array of multicolored splatters. "Guys, I finished rebuilding the house that Gorgon Heap destroys in the Veterinarian's Hospital tale."

"That's a relief," says Kermit. "So at least all the sets are ready to go again?"

"Well, not exactly," Beauregard says, blinking. "The penguins and I only just finished painting everything with a fresh coat."

Scooter gulped. "When will it all be dry?"

"How's Thursday?"

Kermit shakes his head. "We can't wait till then. Take a look out there: The reader's already got the book in hand."

Statler leans in to Waldorf and says with a smirk, "I always thought watching the Muppets perform was about as much fun as watching paint dry. Now we'll get to compare in real time!" The old men guffaw.

"Hey, frog!" Kermit turns to see Miss Piggy standing behind him, wearing a plush pink robe and holding her dirndl costume. "Did the Prada replacement for this abomination arrive yet? Because if you think *moi* is going to tarnish her image yet again by wearing—"

But the last part of the sentence is cut off when Scooter checks his watch and lets out a little yelp. "It's time! Places, everyone! Places!"

The Muppets scurry to and fro, taking final looks in the mirror and finding their starting spots on the various sets. Once everyone is where they need to be, Kermit turns to Scooter and says, "As soon as you rap your knuckles on your clipboard, I'll step up on this wooden chair and say my first line from the prologue."

"Sure thing, boss. I'm just waiting for the cue."

"Oh, right. The cue." Kermit turns to look out at you.

Yes, *you*, whose eyeballs are reading these words.

"Hi ho!" He waves a green hand in your direction. "So actually, friend, we need *you* to make this happen. I mean, when you think about it, it's all because of you and your imagination that we're here in the first place." The lights dim and a hush falls. "So as soon as you flip back to page one, or return this book to the library, or pass it to someone else to read, the Muppets will be back in action." He glances around him at the expectant faces of every shape and shade and species, eager to entertain. "We're ready whenever you are."

Everyone waits to play the music.

Everyone waits to light the lights.

Kermit smiles. "It's time to get things started!"

For my dearest guanajos, Kai and Isaac.
And for Javier, the most
wonderful of weirdos—EFJ

To Ozma, Madeline, and Amy.
. . . and they blessed him with
happiness, ever after—OR

Copyright © 2018 by Disney/Muppets. All rights reserved. Published by
Penguin Workshop, an imprint of Penguin Random House LLC, 345 Hudson Street,
New York, New York 10014. PENGUIN and PENGUIN WORKSHOP
are trademarks of Penguin Books Ltd, and the W colophon is a trademark of
Penguin Random House LLC. Printed in the USA.

Library of Congress Control Number: 2018016068

ISBN 9780451534385   10 9 8 7 6 5 4 3 2 1

MEET THE CLASSICS

FAIRY TALES
FROM
THE BROTHERS GRIMM